THE FOUNTAINS OF TIME

A Ghost Story

by David Phillips

Cover: Quex Park, Birchington, Kent - photo by the author.

ONE

Jennifer Sereni
c/o Simon & Schuster, Inc
1230 Avenue of the Americas,
New York,
NY 10020
U.S.A

April 3rd, 2007

Dear Robin Glass,

Undying Flame, A Biography of Hédi Gela

I have been commissioned by Simon and Schuster to write a biography of Hédi Gela for publication in 2010, and as her friend and colleague up to the time of her demise I would very much appreciate the opportunity of meeting with you and recording your valuable recollections of this fine actress and the work you did together on the BBC 1967 television serial, 'The Fountains of Time'.

I understand from your agent that you have been approached before during the past forty

years by various writers of magazine and newspaper articles anxious for you to expose details
of your 'relationship' with Hédi and quite rightly
you have been reluctant to cooperate with such
people, but I want to assure you that my biography is to be a serious assessment of the actress's
life and work and not a prurient exploitation of
her, or your, private life. I enclose copies of my
first book, 'Sappho in European Cinema' (2003),
and my 2006 biography of the opera diva, Claudio
Muzio, 'Vissi d'arte' with – excuse immodesty! –
press reviews so that you may assess my capabil-
ities to tackle a not so very different heroine.

I will be arriving in London early next
month to begin ten weeks of extensive research
which will include visiting Hédi's friends, homes,
workplaces etc and wonder if we could meet for
lunch at the apartment I have taken at 17d Cheyne
Walk where I will be based for the next few
months. I cook a pretty mean steak! – or of course
anywhere else that would acceptable to you.

The premise of 'Undying Flame' will be my
complete conviction that the art of Hédi Gela has
been scandalously neglected over the past forty
years and while I believe her most significant
work to be the three movies she made in France
for Jean-Pierre Melville, I consider that your
memories of the final weeks you shared with Hédi
in that BBC production will form a significant part
of my biography. As her last friend, and also one of

the last people to see her alive, I would be most grateful if you could spare me some of your time so that I can give of my best in this important work.

I very much look forward to hearing from you,

Yours sincerely,
Jennifer Sereni

'Fountains'
9 Bluebell Lane
Kingsbridge
Devon
TQ7 2BY

24th April, 2007

Dear Jennifer Sereni,

Many thanks for your letter and copies of your books, especially the excellent Muzio biography. Your reviews are well deserved: it was actually Hédi who introduced me to the pleasures of classical music in 1967 and I have been a fan of this particular diva's recordings for many years. I found your book absolutely fascinating and, yes, I can see a number of parallels between Claudio and Hédi's ill-fated lives.

I am delighted that you have been commissioned to tackle Hédi Gela's biography and am perfectly happy to help you in any way that I can.

However loud alarm bells did begin to ring when I saw the word 'relationship', albeit in inverted commas, nestling in your second paragraph! Hédi and I for the few weeks we worked together on 'The Fountains of Time' for the BBC were colleagues but I must state categorically, as I have often done before, that I did not have sexual relations with Hédi Gela – and if that sounds a bit Clintonesque let me say that at the time I was happily married to my first wife and absolutely nothing of a physical nature went on between the subject of your biography and myself. I feel it necessary to clear the air like this so that you are under no illusions that, sentimental old fellow that I have since become, I might suddenly collapse under your laser-like questioning and confess to a searing sexual encounter with Hédi which will provide your biography with the rocket boost your publishers would obviously appreciate.

Now there's a problem! For my sins I have become rather crocked with arthritis and my grouch of a doctor would have seven fits if I suddenly decided to waltz off to London without his say-so. Did you know I once had a flat just off the Embankment where you will be staying? I would have liked to visit that part of Town once again but if you wish to interview me I'm afraid that you will have to come here to Devon, which let me say is absolutely gorgeous at this time of the year. I have no idea how long you wish to interview me for but I suppose a day will be enough won't it? Unfortunately my humble abode is – intentionally – too small for me to put up guests but there is an excellent inn, 'The Bear', a few hundred yards from my cottage, where you will be made very welcome if you decide to stay the extra day.

Hopefully this will fit in with your plans and I very much look forward to seeing you sometime next month.

Best wishes,
Robin Glass

Re Hedi Gela Biography

Jennifer Sereni

To: Robin Glass

Hi Robin,

Thank you so much for your kind and helpful letter. I could get down to see you by train on the May 15, May 18 or the May 26 – you choose. If I arrive at say, 10.30 and you allow me to spend the day with you – lunch at 'The Bear's on me — I could get back to London in the afternoon and leave you in peace.

All best wishes,
Jennifer

Re Hedi Gela Biography

Robin Glass

To: Jennifer Sereni

Dear Jennifer,

The 18th May would suit me best I think. If you give me a call on 0702463838 ten minutes before your train arrives in Kingsbridge I'll be happy to pick you up from the station. The taxis here always take you the long way round (like in New York!) and my run is much prettier.

Best wishes,
Robin

Some prefatory notes in respect of my interview with actor, Robin Glass dictated 5/18/07

My train arrived at Kingsbridge Station — a dead ringer for a movie set from 'Random Harvest' — at about 10.15 am and Robin was waiting on the platform to greet me. Although he is in his mid-sixties and supposedly suffers from arthritis he looks extremely fit and walks without a cane. He is tanned, lean, remarkably handsome for his age and appears exactly how I imagined a British movie star might look. However I was very pleasantly surprised at how normal and unassumingly he turned out to be: there was no side, and no playing the big star or great English stage actor. This was refreshing and fairly unique among the – admittedly limited – number of famous actors and movie stars I have met.

'Jennifer?'

'Robin Glass! I'm so very pleased to meet you. You look exactly like your photograph in Spotlight.'

'Gawd, you must be star-struck, that is a very young picture of me.'

'You seem pretty fit, I was expecting a horribly bent old man!'

'Thanks very much! Here, let me take your bags.'

'Can you manage?'

'Not feeling too decrepit this morning. Heavens, what have you got in these? You look as though you've come for the week.'

'I know Robin, I'm so sorry, I got all this extra paperwork at the last moment and simply had to bring it along.'

If the station was like a miniature of one of those models kids buy for their train kits then Robin's jalopy was straight out of a kid's picture book: a tiny green bubble-like auto that looked as if it belonged in a junk yard. I wondered if the guy was on the skids and felt guilty because I had never thought he might be hard up and perhaps I was imposing on his kindness and generosity.

'Hey, what a wonderful old car. It looks as though it needs a key to wind it up.'

'I'll take that as a compliment. I've been the proud owner of my dear old Morris 1000 since I took up driving in my late forties — can't seem to get shot of her. I do actually own a rather larger and smarter car but I thought with the top down and it being a nice day you'd see more of the scenery.'

'Sure!'

'Crossed the pond before?'

'No, this is my first trip to England.'

'And how do you like it so far?'

'Very much indeed — only been here for a few days but I've grown to love the place. The people are so friendly but I also like the English reserve, it's very refreshing after living in New York for the last five years.'

'Great city, New York. I did a David Hare play off-Broadway a few years back. Loved the buzz, loved the stores, loved the New Yorkers, loved everything about the place.'

'OK to visit for a few months maybe but not somewhere you'd want to put down roots if you have any sense.'

'Maybe not. I forgot to ask, how was the journey down?'

I had thought I wouldn't tell Robin about the

creep who made a pass at me on the train because of the ramifications which I don't need to go into with this guy but there is something about him that makes holding back such information seem petty and unnecessary. However I had forgotten about that British sense of humour!

'Yes, the journey was fine apart from being propositioned by some old gent on the train.'

'Blimey! Was he as old as me?'

'Much younger. I told him I was a lesbian.'

'And what did he say to that?'

'He looked at me as though I was a piece of shit.'

'Oh dear, I am sorry. He wasn't so much of a gentleman then.'

'No, but then I am a lesbian.'

'Right!'

'You don't mind my telling you that, Robin?'

'Why should I?'

'Oh, some people can still funny about these things.'

'I've been in show business far too long to be worried by little things like a person's sexuality. I can assure you we've got lots of dykes and faggots poncing about on the stage here in Britain, I sometimes I wonder I got anywhere at all in the business without being a serial shirt-lifter.'

'Excuse me?'

'Only joking Jennifer!'

'I see, the great English sense of irony I've heard so much about.'

'British irony if you please. We mustn't leave out the Welsh, Scottish and Northern Irish, they get terribly upset about being labelled English.'

'I must remember that.'

'You'll have to forgive my puerile sense of humour Jenny, it's got worse as I've grown older. I did actually suspect you might be gay from your resumé.'

'Sappho in European Cinema?'

'It was a bit of a giveaway.'

'Just so long as you don't think that I hate men or hate you or anything gross like that.'

'That would be rather starting off on the wrong foot, wouldn't it?'

'I want you to know that I'm very much looking forward to our interview, Robin.'

'Me too!'

So that was a relief now I don't need to worry that a) Robin will make a pass at me while I'm here, and b) I shan't need to discuss my background when trying to prize sensitive stuff from him. He is an excellent driver, not flashy or out to impress me that an old wreck can still cut the mustard – the car, not Robin! He drove quite slowly letting me appreciate the wonderful countryside of Devon that, at this time of the year, as he promised was unbelievable.

'You were absolutely right, Robin, this scenery is amazing!'

'It is lovely: wonderful colour of those horse-chestnut leaves with the sun shining through them.'

'And these incredible winding lanes, humped back bridges and slow-moving rivers – right out of 'Wind in the Willows'. Just look at that quaint little church!'

'St. Marks of Kingsbridge.'

'So do you attend services there?'

'I do sometimes, I'm rather fond of church music, although I have to confess I'm really a closet agnostic. Don't like the dogma of religion and don't care for the logical inconsistencies they try to shove down one's throat.'

'But you still like to go to church in spite of this?'

'As Pascal says, believing in God is the better bet. I don't actually like pure atheism very much – strikes me that all these very brainy blokes that tell us we're such fools to believe in God seem to forget that if God does exist he's probably going to be considerably more intelligent than the lot of them put together, so all their theorising comes down to so much hot air.'

'You seem very well adjusted to me, Robin. No hang-ups and happy to be yourself.'

'Yes, I've been lucky and always had the gift of contentment. As an Italian-American, you'll be a Roman Catholic?'

'Lapsed.'

'Just as well with you being gay.'

'Sorry?'

'Doesn't the Pope regard homosexuality as a mortal sin?'

'Yes, I'm rather afraid he does.'

'I just wondered if it worried you.'

'I get by.'

'And here we are!'

My fears that Robin might be on his beam-ends were quite unfounded because he pulled up at the most beautiful thatched cottage imaginable with extensive wooded grounds, heated pool etc – the guy must be worth a million!

'My God, what an incredible home you have, Robin!'

'Picture-book enough for you, Jennifer?'

'Like a cottage in an English fairly story!'

'British fairy story, Jennifer!'

'Does this lovely place have a name?'

'I never bother using it in the address but actually it's called, 'The Fountains of Time'.

TWO

OK, now you don't mind if I tape all this?
I've been interviewed before.

Of course you have, but I want you to know that anything I record will only be used for the purposes of writing my biography. Don't worry that any of this stuff is going to end up in some crummy TV documentary.
I wouldn't think that at all likely.

Such a nice garden you have here, Robin.
I bribe an old boy from the village who comes in twice a week. He does what he likes and I let the old sod get on with it. You don't mind squeezing into my rather over-cluttered study? I thought it would be the best place for us to sift through so many memories. Close the French windows if it's too draughty for you.

No, I'm fine; it's a great view. Are all these manuscripts, the plays and films you've appeared in?
Pretty well a complete collection I should think, maybe a few commercials and the occasional money-grabbing soap appearance might not have

been considered worth keeping.

Jeez, you've worked hard!
And I've enjoyed most of it. There's quite a bit of documentation about the TV serial of 'The Fountains of Time' that might be of interest to you – if I can lay my hands on the stuff.

Can't wait! Have you lived in Devon for long, Robin?
About twenty years. I bought the cottage as a nest egg from the extremely generous fees my agent wrestled from Lord Lew Grade for acting the lead in a television detective series, 'Parsons' Patch'. My second wife, Lili, and I had intended to retire here but she found someone else so I moved in on my own.

Gosh, I'm sorry.
Please don't be, I was perfectly happy with the arrangement.

'Parsons' Patch', did we get that in the States?
I rather think you did. As I remember, it survived for three inglorious seasons on your Masterpiece Theatre show. Alistair Cooke fronted that, didn't he? Though in all modesty I have to say that my character as Detective Chief Superintendent Jack Parsons appeared in very few actual masterpieces. But it was well enough written and thankfully repeats and DVD sales keep this place going.

Great! So you don't need to work anymore?

No, don't have to do that, thank God. Unofficially I chucked it all in a couple of years ago, primarily for health reasons, but I was getting on, I was well past sixty – nearer bloody seventy now! Attractive offers of work were becoming few and far between and really I'd had enough of acting: I was no longer enjoying it. It seemed the right time to call it a day.

Shame, you're an excellent actor. There was a tremendous movie on TV in New York I caught before I flew over here, with you and Christopher Lee –
'Curse of the Mummy's Hand' – 1973. I can't imagine what you thought of it. Total balls in my opinion, and that's being extremely polite.

God no! I'm not over fond of horror movies but made an exception with that one because you were starring in it: the handsome archaeologist who falls in love with the High Priest's mummified daughter, I was captivated! You know how we adore vintage British movies in the States.
How old are you, if you don't mind me asking?

Twenty-eight.
I think you're patronising me, Jennifer. You don't have to compliment my work. I might be going gaga but I have a very good idea of my abilities as an actor.

I wouldn't dream of patronising you, Robin. You must know how fond we Americans are of British

actors, even if we do occasionally cast you as bad guys when we hire you for our movies. You were an extremely accomplished actor, you might not be a huge star in the States but people who know about movies remember you, and that's no bull-shit. There are several web sites with informa-tion about Robin Glass. Now let's see - 'Parsons' Patch' - I must have something here about that show.

Heavens, is that enormous file all about me?

Yes sir. I got my assistant to Google you. Afraid I haven't had a chance to go through too much of this stuff yet.

You have an assistant?

Sure: David Heneker.

He does your donkey work?

Why not? He gets well paid for it. You actors have stand-ins that do your work while you sip Mar-tini's in your trailers, don't you?

I'm flattered that you, or your assistant, have taken so much trouble over me.

When I said your contribution to my book was likely to be important, Robin, I wasn't piss-ing you around. I have some very nice material from Hungry: unpublished letters from Hédi to her family and friends she wrote to in Budapest while she was living in London; diaries she kept as a schoolgirl. But you're the key player as far as I'm concerned, without your co-operation I don't

think I would want to write this biography.
I hope you consider my contribution will be worth your while.

I love doing the research on my books, hate writing them!
Yes, I often disliked acting on stage and filming on location but I always loved rehearsing in draughty church halls or flyblown youth clubs.

When and where were you were born, Robin?
In the middle of a German air-raid, on the 31st of March, 1942 at Lewisham General Hospital not far from our rather modest house in Sydenham, South London, then an extremely depressing suburb whose only real claim to fame was being home to the Crystal Palace.

I've heard of them, they're a soccer club.
God no, I'm not talking about bloody football; I'm referring to the real Crystal Palace. It was originally an actual palace made of glass – absolutely massive, where they held concerts and exhibitions and firework displays. It burnt down in November, 1936. My mother remembers looking out of her back-bedroom window one evening and seeing the sky lit up like day. She thought at first it was a pyrotechnical exhibition but then she heard the crashing glass and the sound of fire engines.

Right, and so what did your father do?
My father was chief clerk at a produce brokers near Fenchurch Street in the City of London. My

mother worked part-time as a shop assistant a few streets away from the terraced house where I was brought up with my two elder sisters, Jane and Elizabeth. The street where we lived was nothing to shout about but the road parallel to the back of us had larger, grander houses whose gardens abutted ours. One I remember was the local Conservative Club, another – it seems extraordinary to me now – was a children's drama school.

OK, let me stop you there for a second and ask you what you were like as a child.
I was a nice little boy: sweet and innocent, not overburdened in the brain department I suppose, well, not a swot, but lots of solid commonsense, sensitive and artistic, shy but surprisingly ambitious in my own quiet way. I realised from the beginning that I came from relatively humble stock but always felt that I would make my mark in life. I wanted above everything else to make my family proud of me.

You certainly achieved that!
My father wanted me to become a stockbroker!

But wasn't he immensely proud of you when you appeared on TV?
I suppose he must have been. He was a rather taciturn man and never said much, never showed a great deal of emotion. People didn't in those days – something to do with the War I suppose.

You were saying there was a drama school at the

back of your yard?

Incredibly, yes: a temple to the arts stuck incongruously in the centre of a resolutely working-class district. It was totally magical. As a child I would peer over the garden wall at the kids acting in their little open-air tableaux: miniature kings and queens and knights on hobbyhorse chargers, or tiny characters in Shakespeare plays. I remember a production of A Midsummer Night's Dream where fairies with tissue paper wings danced at the bottom of the garden.

Fantastic! And that's how it all started for you?

It didn't take me long to get the acting bug and I begged my mother to enrol me in a Saturday morning dance and movement class at 2/6d a session – in US currency that would be about 50 cents at 1950s prices – quite a lot of money in those days to spend on a child's whim. I loved it all though, came out of my shell, worked very hard and at nine years old was the complete star.

What were your fellow students like?

Very much as you'd expect: spoilt little girls sent by their mothers to improve their deportment; reluctant boys, terrified of being called sissies who would much rather have been playing football or cricket; genuine sissies who wouldn't have fitted into normal schooling. I was fairly unique I suppose in that without being in the least bit effeminate, I actually enjoyed every aspect of acting and stagecraft. I worked hard because it didn't

seem like work to me, everything was new and fun
to do.

Were your professors any good?

Professors! It was a very small school but surprising good in its way although our Principal, Miss
Molly Clackett was one of the old time music
and drama teachers. Reputed to have once been
a 'Gaiety Girl' in her distant youth, her enthusi-
asms lay with the heroes of that golden age: Noel
Coward, Henry Ainley, Sir Gerald du Maurier –
the whole Twenties crowd. That she had flapped,
Bunny-hopped, Lindy-hopped and Charleston-ed
with the best of them could not be doubted; that
she failed to entirely embrace later developments
in the popular arts was made patently obvious by
her rather selective curriculum.

She wasn't into 'The Method'?

No indeed she wasn't – probably never heard of
it — she had her own methods. These were practical rather than overly imaginative. In assuming
the role of a tramp, or bum as you would call him,
it was only necessary to pretend to be a tramp; to
look like a tramp and to speak and do things that
tramps do. She would dirty your face with burnt
cork, paint out a couple of front teeth, give you
an old coat to wear two sizes too large or three
sizes too small and tell you to get on with it. You
had only to walk with a rolling or restricted gait,
muttering idiocies to yourself to secure the full
approbation of Molly's judgement. The Stanislav-

skyian or Chekhovian idea of imagining that you actually were a tramp, to inwardly invent a whole scenario of past occurrences that had made you into a tramp, and to fully empathise with the subject being played would have seemed very strange to her. If you acted, you pretended – it was as simple as that.

And you built a career on this teaching?
Why not? Music and Dance were also rather old fashioned: Molly's knowledge and love for the polite musical comedies of an earlier era could not encompass spunky Fifties shows like 'Damn Yankees' and 'The Pyjama Game'. She considered these American masterpieces to be the loud and vulgar end of a great period that had fully matured with the works of Irvin Berlin, Jerome Kern, Cole Porter and Ivor Novello. Even a punchy and effective piece such as Irvin Berlin's, 'Annie get your Gun' she regarded as an aberration and a sad example of a once great man's declining powers.

Now there's a great show.
Yes it was – and is. Perhaps I make Molly sound like an out of touch old charlatan, taking her pupils' Saturday shillings for two hours of airy-fairy crap, but nothing could be further from the truth. She was an excellent teacher of children, always keeping them interested, and a strict disciplinarian. She would chuck out of her classes inattentive or over-boisterous children, or anyone she thought had a below zero talent factor. She hated ama-

teurism in any shape or form. The general perception in the Fifties and Sixties was for theatrical managements to see young actors as glorified pop singers, in other words foul-mouthed tearaways or arty-farty beatnik types. This may have been true in some cases but you will always find the most accomplished actors have achieved their success by solid hard work and iron discipline. When I made a film, 'The Terror of the Tongs' in 1959, Rueben Wallace, the director suddenly decided that my character would need to sweep the heroine off her feet in an impromptu polka and so he arranged for a morning's tuition so that I would be up to performing this stunt in the Victorian ballroom scene. When I told him that this would be unnecessary as I had learned most of the Nineteenth Century ballroom dances at the age of ten and was reasonably confident that I could perform a polka in front of the camera without going arse-over-tit, he immediately demanded a demonstration. They ran some music and I swept my would-be tutor around Lord Carson's gothic ballroom like that Fred and Ginger scene in 'Swing Time', to the applause of the film crew and a muttered, "No one likes a smart-arse", from dear old Rueben.

I shall look out for 'The Terror of the Tongs' when I get back to the States.

It was all due to Molly's insistence on mastering the basics. She never spoke down to children or babied her pupils in any way, treating us more like Rada students than the dumb kids we actually were. I think I must have been her favourite pupil. After the last student had rushed out of her shabby rehearsal room she would wind up the ancient gramophone and we would have one last dance together before she would kiss me lightly on my cheek and send me off home.

God, how romantic! You must have been a fabulous pupil to teach.
I obviously impressed my instructors because after a couple of terms I was awarded a scholarship to attend full-time. I was a nice looking boy, fresh-faced and appealing. It wasn't long before Molly began to farm me out to the Agencies and I began to get paid work. Newspaper and magazine ads to start with – I was a Fifties Persil Boy.

Purcell?
Not Purcell the composer, Persil the soap powder! They would show two boys, one with a gleaming white shirt washed in Persil and the other urchin with a grubby grey shirt washed with Brand X.

And which boy did you play?
Both of them! I began to get small radio parts and walk-ons in films and TV, then I would get to say a few lines and my roles would grow appreciably larger.

What was your break-through part as a child?
It was, of course, 'The Fountains of Time'.

Hey, just one moment, surely that was taped by the BBC in 1967 when you would have been twenty-five – you played the Fountain Spirit with Hédi Gela as your sister?
I also played 11 year-old Michael Summerwood in their first adaptation of 'The Fountains of Time'— a six-part BBC Television serial broadcast live in 1954.

Good God!
I'm sure this must all be in the huge file you have on me that your David thingummy downloaded from the Internet.

I'm so embarrassed! Jeez, I am sorry, Robin, I really should have spent more time looking through your resumé, but I only got all this stuff faxed through to me yesterday evening.
Please don't apologize, Jennifer, after all you're writing a biography about Hédi Gela, not me!

I don't want you to think I'm some sort of two-bit literary carpetbagger who can't be bothered to check out a few simple facts. 'The Fountains of Time'! Seems this kids' show has more relevance than I could ever have dreamed of. So there were in fact two BBC serials, one in 1954 and one in 1967 – and you were in both of them, how extra-ordinary.
Have you read the 1948 novel they were based on?

Absolutely not! I have a copy of the 1967 tele-

vision script somewhere, which I've dipped into, and there must be some biographical information about the author. Do you think I need to go through the book as well?

Hmm...

OK, OK, so I'll read the damned book.
I have a beautiful signed edition that the author, Adrian Mackinder gave me at Lime Grove studios in 1954 when he was visiting the set. Would you like to look at it?

Love to! Let's see now, It says here that Mackinder was born in 1879 so the old guy must have seemed pretty decrepit to you at the time?
I thought he was incredibly ancient – smelled of pipe tobacco and expensive cologne – although the book had only been published five or six years before I met him, in 1948, I think by that time he'd stopped writing. 'The Fountains of Time' was his best book and biggest seller although the first reviews weren't so great. He snipped out this horrific gem from 'John O'London's Weekly' which he left in the book to encourage me to overcome possible adversity and setbacks in my future acting career:'from flame and iron, steel is forged!'

John O' London's Weekly
23rd February, 1948

'The Fountains of Time'

Adrian Mackinder, (Eyre and Spottiswoode 8/6d)

Adrian Mackinder's previous novel for children, 'The Madcap Pirates' was a firm Christmas favourite several years ago and it is always a pity when a new work fails to approach the élan and vigour of the old. 'The Fountains of Time' is an extraordinary departure from the frolicsome pirates of yester-year and its dark and eerie qualities will appeal to only the most sophisticated and questioning children, if such prodigies exist these days. The tale, which one cannot help feeling must have been more enjoyable to write than to read, leads a young brother and sister to a haunted manor house in Devon where the Fountains of the title and the lure of a long lost treasure inveigle the children into adventures set in an historical past that begin well but end in not a little confusion. An episode where the children prevent Captain Blood from stealing the Crown Jewels in the Tower of London is exciting enough but is marred by insinuations of Blood's amatory relationship with his paramour which I would have thought unsuitable for a novel of this kind. Luridly violent episodes portray the siege of Sidney Street in 1911 and a supposed invasion of the West Country by Nazi spies invokes scenes of horrific torture that frankly turn the stomach. A final tableau, seemingly involving a Christ-like figure and strongly suggestive that Our Saviour did indeed include South Devon in His brief Ministry on this earth, verges on the blasphemous and the denouement set in the dawn of history when the Fountains were apparently constructed by visitors from a distant galaxy stretch the bounds of belief to snapping point. Mr. Mackinder's plodding reliance on Jungian symbolism to achieve his effects would hardly be forgivable in an adult work of fiction but to foster such absurdities on a light-hearted children's romance goes beyond all reason. 'The Fountains of Time' is a sad but imperative example to those misguided enough to believe that children should be dragged by their ears into an adult world that has no respect, liking or love for the certainties and beauties of childhood innocence.

Wilfred Nevinson

That's a real bummer. If I ever get a review like for one of my books I'll murder the guy. How did the old boy take it?
Water off a duck's back if he had any sense. Anyway it didn't do Adrian Mackinder any harm at all: 'The Fountains of Time' was a fairly solid success and went on to become his most famous book. If 'The Madcap Pirates' and all his other children's stories have sunk without trace, 'The Fountains of Time' was in print until the 1970s I believe, and can still be found in the odd charity shop – I think you call them thrift shops – it's immortality of a sort I suppose.

Did you read it as a child, I mean, before you acted in it?

We had one of your lovely Carnegie Libraries in Sydenham, near to where I lived and I remember borrowing the novel from the children's section so I was familiar with the story before I began acting in the television serial.

It's funny the kids not minding the symbolism and religious imagery that reviewer got so worked up about. Do you suppose it flew straight over their heads?

Oh yes, Patrick Keith, who adapted the book for the BBC's 1954 production more or less ignored all the heavy stuff and quite properly concentrated on the intriguing and exciting aspects of the story. Like the works of Lewis Carroll, 'The Fountains of Time' can be read on several different levels and I'm certain the novel had been written by Mackinder to appeal to different readerships. When you make an adaptation for television you have to decide which of the books you're going to show and since in 1954 the target was a Sunday afternoon children's audience, Keith went for the fun, exciting stuff. That's not to say the original novel is in any way inferior to the show we were making.

CHAPTER ONE

An Unexpected Letter!

"May I have another piece of toast please, Mummy," asked Michael, his hand already stealing towards the toast rack in anticipation of a favourable reply.

"Don't be such a greedy pig!" his younger sister Susan laughed, "You've had at least four slices already!"

"Not four, three."

"Very well, just one more, Michael, but make that piece the last one," smiled Mrs. Summerwood, "you've got a long journey to Coniston to begin this morning and we don't want to keep stopping because you feel car sick."

"But I'm never car sick," protested Michael, "I have the constitution of an ox."

"And an appetite like one!" growled his father glancing up briefly from behind his newspaper at the rapidly diminishing pieces of toast in the rack.

It was the first day of August and both Michael and Susan were very excited because they were going to spend the next three weeks holidaying among the mountains of the Lake District. Their Father, an ex-Sunderland Flying-boat Captain in the Royal Air Force, had been based in Cumbria during the war and had told them many thrilling stories about flying over the wild and beautiful country with its towering peaks, lush green valleys and icy waterfalls. Now as the children finished breakfast with the morning sun streaming invitingly in through the dining-room window, they could talk of nothing but the long motorcar drive that would take them from the pretty village in Kent where they lived to the magnificent vales and mountains of Coniston.

"How long will it take us to drive there, Daddy," enquired Susan wondering how many of her favourite ghost story books she should take to pass away the long hours on the road.

"Well, let me see," said Father, "with a normal car and a fair wind behind us I should say about ten or eleven hours, but with our old jalopy I think you can safely double that."

"That's not fair!" protested Michael, "our lovely maroon Riley Merlin is not an 'old jalopy'– and I've seen her do at least sixty when there was no wind behind her at all."

"But that was downhill, Michael," said Daddy with a serious look on his face, "if you look at a map you'll find the road to the Lake District is all uphill!"

"Anyway" laughed Michael, "I don't care how long the journey takes, the main thing is that we have three full weeks to explore the great houses and castles in the area to assess their treasure hunting and adventure seeking possibilities."

"Treasure hunts!" groaned Mother, "that's all you children ever seem to think of these days."

"And ghost hunts!" said Susan excitedly. "Where there are old houses and castles and hidden treasure there are always ghosts roaming about as well."

"Castles?" said Father, finally putting down his newspaper, "What castles? You won't find many castles where we're going, my dear children, or great houses, haunted or otherwise."

"No castles where there might be treasure to be discovered?" said Michael disappointedly.

"And no ghosts flitting about in stately mansions?" asked Susan with a pained look on her face.

"We're holidaying in the Lake District in England, not Bavaria in Germany, where you certainly can see castles perched on mountain tops. When I flew over Coniston and Ullswater during the war I don't remember seeing many mountains with castles stuck on top of them, or stately homes for that matter either!"

"Do stop teasing the children, Father, and read this letter that has just arrived."

Mother, who had been quietly opening the morning's post looked worried as she handed the letter across to Daddy and while he began to read the children watched and saw his face became ever more serious until he looked very concerned indeed.

"Blast!"

He rose from the table with the letter still in his hand then strode off into the study and closed the door behind him with something of an ill-tempered bang.

"What's the matter, Mummy," said Susan, her eyes wide with surprise.

"Some rather bad news, I'm afraid, children. You'll have to wait until Daddy has finished telephoning and then I'm sure he'll tell you all about it."

As Mother gathered up the breakfast things, Michael and Susan could hear Father's raised voice coming from behind the stout oak door of the study. Daddy so rarely became ill-tempered about anything that the children stared silently at each other wondering what on earth this sudden crisis could be all about. After what seemed an age he finally emerged mopping his brow with a handkerchief, still clutching that letter in his hand.

"Come into the study, everyone, I have something rather important to tell you."

Mother ushered the children quickly in and they stared worriedly at Daddy's glum face, dreading what he was about to say. He took a deep breath and tried to smile.

"It's bad news, I'm afraid. We shall have to postpone our holiday to the Lake District."

"Oh no!" cried Susan, tears beginning to

prick at her eyes.

Michael said nothing, realizing that there must be a very good reason for Father's awful announcement.

"Something rather unexpected and serious has occurred, children which I'm afraid to say is even more important than our holidays. A good friend of mine has unfortunately got himself into some kind of trouble and I must do my best to help him."

"Who is this friend?" demanded Michael wondering what sort of friend a person would be who could be responsible for ruining a family's summer holiday.

"He's a chap called Craig Martin, an old wartime chum of mine from the R.A.F. who now lives in France, near Paris. We flew together in the Sunderlands; he was my navigator, my friend and a thoroughly good fellow. It seems that he has got into trouble with the French police and been arrested."

"Gosh, what for?" said Susan excitedly.

"I'd rather not tell you for the moment," said her father, looking at his daughter rather crossly, "and you mustn't ask me again. I will say that the charges against Craig are grave ones but knowing the man as I do I am quite certain that he is innocent and that when everything is sorted out he will be released from prison without a stain on his character."

"And are you going to France to defend him

in court, Father?' asked Michael.

Mr. Summerwood was a family solicitor with a small office in the village where they lived. Most of his cases seemed to Michael to be about rather boring matters like signing passport forms for people and writing wills for irascible old ladies who always wanted to change them afterwards. As far as he knew very few criminals had ever asked Father to represent them in exciting court cases of murder or jewel robberies.

"Craig Martin has a young family; his wife died some months ago and your mother and I must look after his children and I must do my best to free him from custody."

"But can't we come too?" cried Susan, the postponement of her holiday in Coniston almost forgotten at the prospect of a new and even more exciting adventure set in a romantic part of France.

"Unfortunately that will not be possible, children. Pat's house is far too small for us all to put up in and your mother and I will be too busy working on my friend's case to look after you."

"Then what is going to happen to us?" asked Michael looking at his sister anxiously as he suddenly felt a wave of panic begin to stir inside him.

"Now, I have telephoned your Uncle Philip and Aunt Julie in Monckton, South Devon and they have very kindly agreed to put you up for two or three weeks."

"Two or three weeks!" exclaimed Susan, "but that's simply ages!"

"It will soon pass, Susan," said her mother gently, "and then we can all go to the Lake District for our holidays again just as we have arranged."

"But we don't know Uncle Philip and Aunt Julie," said Michael frowning, "we've never met them before."

"That's certainly true!" smiled Father, "they've lived for most of their lives in Kenya and have come home to retire by the sea."

"Retire!" snorted Michael, "then they must both be positively ancient!"

"Oh, really, Michael" scolded Mummy, "they're not at all ancient. They are the same age as me and Daddy, now you don't think we're ancient do you?"

"Well . . ." said Michael uncertainly, "as a matter of fact . . ."

"That's enough, Michael," laughed Daddy, "I realize that you don't know them but I can assure you that my brother and his wife are perfectly nice people. Philip is now the vicar at Monckton Church but until recently he and Julie have spent a large part of their lives in Africa setting up missions, working in hospitals and doing a great deal of good work and it is extremely kind of them to take on two strange children at such short notice."

"We're not strange!" protested Susan.

"Well, not altogether strange." added Michael, "not as strange as Uncle Philip and Aunt

Julie will be to us."

"How on earth do you come to that conclusion?" asked Father with a puzzled expression on his face.

"Everything at their home in Devon will be strange to us but to Uncle Philip and Aunt Julie it will only be us that will be strange."

"I'm sure you'll soon get used to everything. I understand that Monckton Manor is an old and interesting house set on the cliff tops by the sea and I'm sure you will have a tremendous number of adventures while you're there."

At the sound of the word 'adventure' Michael and Susan gave each other brief and secret smiles. If their proper holiday was going to be put off by two or three weeks perhaps a surprise and additional holiday on the South Devon coast in an old and interesting manor house wouldn't be so bad after all!

"But you must be sure not to get under your Aunt and Uncle's feet all day long. Uncle Philip is very busy with his parishioners and spends long hours in his study composing his sermons so he will need lots of peace and quiet." Said Father sternly.

"And Aunt Julie writes a weekly column for a gardening magazine," smiled Mother, "so I don't expect she will want you tearing about and making a lot of noise either!"

"We'll try not to make too much noise," promised Susan, "after all we don't want to frighten away any ghosts that might be drifting about."

"Ghosts don't drift about, Susan," laughed Michael, "they're not like particles of dust floating in the air."

"Well, haunt then. I'm sure Monckton Manor must be full of ghosts and we're bound to see quite a few of them, don't you, Father?"

"Now you're not to make a nuisance of yourself, Susan," said Mother concernedly. "Uncle Philip and Aunt Julie are very passionate about their beliefs and I'm not sure they're that keen on things like spiritualism and ghosts and suchlike. Anyway they won't want you tearing around telling everyone that their beautiful old house is haunted!"

"I'll see Susan behaves herself," said Michael rather self-importantly, "after all I'm sure we're much more likely to meet up with a band of smugglers or jewel thieves trying to use Monckton Manor as a hiding place for stolen contraband or treasure. We'll be far too busy catching criminals or finding masses of hidden treasure to bother with stupid things like ghosts!"

5.0-5.30   **CHILDREN'S TELEVISION**

'The Fountains of Time'
A serial in six parts

from the book by
Adrian Mackinder

Adapted and produced
for television
by Patrick Keith

1. 'The Mystery of Monckton Manor'

Mr Summerwood......................Norman Hughes
Mrs Summerwood................…......Mary Lester
Their children:	
Michael ....…......................Robin Glass
Susan ....…....... ....Anna Lombard
Uncle Philip....................…..... .. ..Claude Irving
Aunt Julie....................…....…..........Blanche Bayless
Stationmaster..................…....William Fleming
Old Daniel...................…......Lawrence England
He-Spirit.................…...…......…......Roger Blake
She-..Billie Gibson

Settings by Gordon Carson

Here's a clipping I kept from the Radio Times–
October, 1954 – my first television credit in the
magazine.

This is a British TV listings publication?

We only had one channel in those days. Of course
I was very excited about being on television. It
was really the beginning of national broadcasting
after the war and everyone learnt as they went
along. It was a tremendously innovative period
for the medium, we were all pioneers. And here's
a photograph from the same magazine of Anna,
the girl who played Susan, sitting with me and
Lawrence England, the lovely drunken ham they

roped in to play the part of Old Daniel.

You look a real cutie, and the girl has a sweet face, who was she?
Anna Lombard was a total pain in the arse: the worst type of stage-school pocket prima donna with an ever-present mother who was always fussing over her and complaining to the director that he wasn't showing her best side.

You didn't at the tender age of twelve fall in love with your co-star then?
Not with Anna Lombard, no.

Ah! But someone else took your fancy?
That, Jennifer, comes a bit later in the story. You will have to postpone your natural curiosity for the appropriate dramatic release of that particular piece of information.

OK, I can wait. 'The Fountains of Time' was filmed on location?
Good Lord, no! It was all done live at the BBC's Lime Grove studio, near Hammersmith, not a million miles from where you're living at the moment.

Dear God, you mean it was broadcast as you acted, in real time?
They didn't have videotape in those days and filming was considered unnecessary and far too expensive.

Weren't you just a little nervous?

Not at all! I had the confidence of youth. No one in our street had a television set in those days, I'd only ever watched the Queen's Coronation on telly in 1953, I had no fear because I didn't understand what I was supposed to be frightened of. Mind you, that couldn't necessarily be said of my fellow cast members.

So how did they react?
In different ways: Lawrence England who played Old Daniel was pissed as a pudding most of the time. Mary Lester, lovely woman, who played my mum, took various pills, the nature of which was not to be enquired into. Norman Hughes, my dad in the serial used to screw himself up to such a pitch that a bucket was provided for him to be sick in off-camera. The rest of us managed to grit our teeth and get on with it. I know the actor, Claude Irving who played my Uncle Philip, was in Special Operations during the war and he used to tell me that being chased around occupied France by the Gestapo wasn't half as frightening as appearing on live television.

You must have rehearsed the serial as if you were doing a stage play.
Early television drama took its techniques not, as one might suppose, from the cinema but almost entirely from the stage. Our television director and stage designer were both theatre men who were recruited by the BBC directly from West End productions. For us actors it was like being in rep.

Rep?

Short for Repertory Theatre. Apart from West End productions British Theatre consisted almost entirely of small companies of actors touring provincial theatres and putting on new plays every week. I did my stint for a couple of years in my late teens: it was gruelling work of a generally poor standard but it's how actors of my generation learnt their craft and earned a living.

Would you say that the 1954 BBC production of 'The Fountains of Time' was a faithful adaptation of the novel?

Oh, I would think so. If I remember correctly author Adrian Mackinder actually collaborated with Patrick Keith on the scripts – there was certainly some input from him because I recall seeing the old boy bustling about the set quite often. Of course in the 1967 version we had videotape that could be edited if we made mistakes and proper-filmed locations, whereas in 1954 we played in front of cardboard props and painted backdrops. Monckton Manor, the main setting of the story, was a 10 x 8 inch photograph set on an easel with a television camera stuck in front of it.

For a story about time-travel and magic it must have been a challenge for the special effects department, how did they cope?

There wasn't a special effects department as such, everything was left to the producer's ingenuity. They had this terrible clichéd effect whereby the passing of time or onset of a magical transformation was always introduced by mixing in a telecine film of drifting white smoke against a black background. You saw the damn thing in every BBC production in the 1950s, it was an all purpose effect that telly people never seemed to tire of.

The cast never complained working with such primitive effects?
It wasn't our place to criticize the technical staff. Anyway it was a useful device, literally a smoke screen, to get us from one scene to the next. The problem with live television was making costume changes and rushing to different scenes in time without tripping over the cables and going arse-over-tit. This filmed insert may have slowed the pace of the drama somewhat but they were a godsend to us hard-pressed actors.
And here we are: 'The Fountains of Time', my original 1954 BBC script for the first episode. Do you see how I studiously underlined my part in red coloured pencil like a real pro?

You loved performing in the serial?
God, it was complete and utter magic!

THREE

"THE FOUNTAINS OF TIME" EPISODE 1.

8. EXT. RAILWAY PLATFORM. TELECINE. DAY

(THE TRAIN PULLS INTO MONCKTON STATION AND MICHAEL AND SUSAN STEP DOWN WITH THEIR SUITCASES FROM THE RAILWAY CARRAGE. THEY LOOK UP AND DOWN THE PLATFORM FOR THEIR AUNT AND UNCLE BUT THE STATION APPEARS TO BE DESERTED. AFTER A FEW MOMENTS OF UNCERTAINTY THEY TRUDGE INTO THE STATIONMASTER'S OFFICE)

9. INT. STATIONMASTER'S OFFICE. STUDIO. DAY

(THE STATIONMASTER IS IN HIS SHIRTSLEEVES AND WHISTLING TO HIMSELF AS HE BREWS UP A POT OF TEA)

STATIONMASTER: Good morning children, what can I do for you?

MICHAEL: We were expecting to be met by our Aunt and Uncle from Monckton Manor.

SUSAN: And there's no one here at all!

STATIONMASTER: Why, you must be Michael and Susan, travelled all the way from London on your own! I'm Gregory Evans the stationmaster, I was told to look out for you.

MICHAEL: We've been on the train for an absolute age.

SUSAN: (LOOKING ENVIOUSLY AT THE STEAMING TEAPOT) Yes, and we're both very tired — and thirsty!

STATIONMASTER: Then perhaps you will do me the great honour of taking a cup of tea with me.

MICHAEL: Yes, please!

SUSAN: Oh, thank you!

STATIONMASTER: Do sit down and make yourselves comfortable. Old Daniel'll be on his way now with the pony and trap if I'm not much mistaken. Your train was five minutes early – now would you believe that! Here, have a biscuit while you're waiting.

MICHAEL: Thank you, but who is Old Daniel?

STATIONMASTER: Old Daniel? Why he's your Uncle's faithful factotum.

SUSAN: What is a factotum?

MICHAEL: He's a sort of servant, isn't he?

STATIONMASTER: Don't think Daniel would like to be thought of as a servant! He's been at Monckton Manor since your Uncle was a boy. Fair runs the place he does, don't know what they'd do without Old Daniel.

MICHAEL: I thought Uncle Philip and Aunt Julie would be in charge at Monckton Manor.

STATIONMASTER: Your Uncle and Aunt are in charge of the place all right but they're much too busy to see to everything that needs doing at the Manor. Why there's the upkeep and cleaning of the house to be undertaken. Old Daniel and his missus look after everything so your uncle can concentrate on ministering to his flock and your aunt can write her gardening columns for them magazines of hers.

MICHAEL: We were told that Monckton Manor is a very large house.

STATIONMASTER: Well you weren't told wrong, Master Michael – it's as big as Manor houses get in these parts I should think.

MICHAEL: Then how can Old Daniel and his wife look after everything? Isn't there too much for them to do?

STATIONMASTER: You're quite right, there is too

much for them to do but if you're a country parson I suppose you can only afford to have so much done.

SUSAN: Is Monckton Manor haunted?

MICHAEL: Oh Susan!

STATIONMASTER: Now where in Heaven's name did you get that idea, miss?

MICHAEL: Don't listen to her, Mr. Evans! Susan's talked of nothing else on the train. Just because Monckton Manor's as old as time itself she thinks the house has got to be haunted!

STATIONMASTER: 'As old as Time itself'. Well, you certainly said something there, Master Michael! I don't know about any ghosts but the Manor is the oldest house in these parts and I can't think of anybody who really knows exactly how old she really is.

SUSAN: Then Monckton Manor must be haunted. How thrilling!

MICHAEL: You are an idiot, Susan! Of course there are no such things as ghosts, are there, Sir?

STATIONMASTER: (GLANCING THROUGH WINDOW) Don't ask me children! Ghosts! How would I know if such things exist? Now here's Old Daniel in the trap, finish up your tea. You can ask him if Monckton Manor is haunted, I'm sure he'll have something to say about it!

10. EXT. RAILWAY STATION. TELECINE. DAY

(OLD DANIEL LOADS THE CHILDREN'S SUIT-
CASES AND HELPS THEM INTO THE TRAP THEN
CLIMBS UP HIMSELF AND THEY START OFF TO-
WARDS MONCKTON MANOR)

11. EXT. PONY AND TRAP. STUDIO. DAY

OLD DANIEL: Haunted, you say! I never heard
of Monckton Manor being haunted before, why
should you think of such a thing?

MICHAEL: Don't take any notice of her, sir; my sister is too fond of reading ghost stories for her own
good.

SUSAN: That's not true!

MICHAEL: You can't see any old house without
imagining a ghost haunts the place!

SUSAN: And you can't see one without thinking
it's chock-full of buried treasure!

OLD DANIEL: Buried treasure, fancy that! Well, I
suppose some old houses might be haunted and
some might have some buried treasure but I think
you'll find Monckton Manor to be something of a
disappointment in both respects.

SUSAN: But the Stationmaster said the house was
very old.

OLD DANIEL: Oh, it's old all right, I never saw an older house in all my life.

MICHAEL: Exactly how old is Monckton Manor, sir?

OLD DANIEL: You don't need to be calling me 'sir'– it's 'Old Daniel', just the same as everyone else calls me. Now Monckton Manor was built on the site of a monastery, one of them old Henry the Eighth got shot of in the Sixteenth Century. The Monastery had been there hundreds of years before that so who knows how long the site has been inhabited?

SUSAN: Gosh, the place is ancient – it must be haunted!

MICHAEL: Really, Susan!

SUSAN: I bet there are lots of ghostly hooded monks disappearing through walls and things!

OLD DANIEL: Now, Mr. Michael, I will say your sister has a very active imagination!

MICHAEL: An over-active imagination I would say. I shouldn't think there would be anything left at Monckton Manor to remind anyone that it was once a monastery.

OLD DANIEL: Well, there are the fountains.

SUSAN: The fountains?

OLD DANIEL: They're in the middle of the rose garden behind the main part of the house; used to be where the monks grew their vegetables and took their afternoon promenades. They are known as 'The Fountains of Time' and some say they go back long before even the monks came to that place.

MICHAEL: Gosh, how exciting!

SUSAN: 'The Fountains of Time!' Why I'm sure they must be enchanted fountains!

OLD DANIEL: Ah Miss, you might be right about that. Ghosts there may or may not be at Monckton Manor but there's certainly something fascinating about them there fountains. Come on, old boy!

Describe your working day to me when you were twelve years old and making the first television series of 'The Fountains of Time' in 1954.
My Dad would wake me up with a cup of tea at about 6.30. I would have breakfast, wash and get dressed by 7.00. Then I would walk with my father to the railway station and we'd take a train to London Bridge. We'd cross the bridge together and he would turn right towards his office in Fenchurch Street and I would go to the Bank tube station and catch a train to Lime Grove or wherever we were working that day.

You travelled alone?

Quite young children travelled by themselves in those days. Times have changed, but at twelve I was considered old enough to see myself across London. I enjoyed it! On the train I would go over my lines or do schoolwork.

You still went to school?

It was the law here then – and still is as far as I know – children working in film, theatre or television were required to attend classes, in my case on Saturdays and Sundays, to make up for lost teaching.

Didn't you find that rather a drag?

Not at all. Because I actually attended a drama school the staff were more than sympathetic and were happy to cut corners to make sure I wasn't overloaded with work.

How did that affect your schooling in general?

I knew I would never be bright enough to go to university. I didn't want to anyway. I dreamed of becoming a professional actor and by the time I was twelve that's precisely what I became. My education was directed to what was considered useful to me in the profession: obviously all aspects of drama, music, dance and stagecraft were pretty well explored. The school was big on History and English Literature, less so on Mathematics and Geography. I'm afraid I've spent the rest of my life catching up on Science. I must have been in

my twenties before I realised the earth travelled
around the sun and why the seasons occurred.

**OK, back to your days shooting, 'The Fountains
of Time'.**
This is all rather boring. Why don't you read my
diary?

You kept a diary as a boy?
I was given a diary as a school project and I've kept
one ever since.

You've always written a diary?
Apart from odd days when I've been ill or too busy,
yes.

**You wrote a diary during the time of your friend-
ship with Hédi Gela in 1967?**
Certainly.

Good God, Robin, I had no idea!
I was going to tell you! I thought you might find it
useful in your researches.

Jeez, I should say so! Where do you keep them all?
Here, along this bottom shelf. As you can see
there's quite a collection. Now, October, 1954 –
this is it!

Monday, 11th October, 1954

Rainy a.m. Breakfast: Boiled egg and soldiers. Finished English HK on train. History HK on tube plus

learnt lines.

What is 'HK'?

Homework!

Did excellent first scene with Mr Irving and Miss Bayless. Lawrence told me rude joke which I didn't quite understand. Cheese sandwich and Smiths crisps for lunch. Lawrence went to pub. Rehearsed fountain scene in afternoon. Anna very silly as usual. Mr Keith said I was v. good. Met Billie Gibson who is playing lots of different parts later on. She's a dish. Met Dad at Bank Station and we looked at Keil Kraft turbo-prop in Model Shop at London Bridge. Hoping to buy it this week. Sausages for tea. Listened to 'The Goon Show'– v. funny then went to bed.

Tuesday, 12th October, 1954

A nice sunny day but quite cold. Breakfast. Bovril on toast (3 slices). Read most of Henry V on train for HK. Not a bad play really. Learnt lines for transformation scene. Bet Anna hasn't learnt hers yet but I've got most to say. Sat around all of the morning because Mr Keith said he had to spend extra time with adults as they weren't as good as the youngsters!!!! 2 sausage rolls and doughnut for lunch. Excellent. Lawrence went to pub (again!) Did more work on fountain scene in afternoon with Billie G. Lush!! Dad and I looked in model shop again. It's still there. Had toad in hole for tea. Told mum I'd already had sausages today (and yesterday!). Listened to 'Take it from here' on the radio. Not as funny as last week but still pretty good. Had bath and went to bed.

Who's Lawrence?
He played Old Daniel and was my special friend in the cast.

Right.

Wednesday, 13th October, 1954

Overcast but warmer than yesterday. Breakfast. Cornflakes (2 bowls). Started essay on Henry V on train for HK. No lines to learn today! Billie, Douglas, Anna and I went by coach to Merton Park to film outside location shots for episodes 2 & 3. Billie gave me one of her salad sandwiches which she made herself. Scrumptious! I gave her one of my cheese sandwiches but I think she lost it. Dad bought me Keil Kraft turbo-prop out of my wages. It's fantastic!! We started to make it on the kitchen table straightway and I went to bed at 10.30!!!'

May I take some of these back to London with me?
Can't imagine why you'd want to read such callow rubbish – oh, of course you mean the diaries I wrote when I was working with Hédi in '67, the sensational stuff?

I'm sorry I didn't mean to appear too eager.
That's all right, Jennifer, I absolutely understand, after all you're writing a biography of Hédi Gela, not me. I'm surprised you want to hear anything at all about my life in 1954.

I'm not bored with all this material you're giving me about the first BBC production of 'The Fountains of Time', Robin, in fact it's fascinating and it's helping me to understand the background of the 1967 version of the book. It's incredible that you were in both, playing different parts and working with all kinds of different people. Please believe me, Robin, when I start to get bored with what you're telling me I'll let you know.
Fine! As you can see so far all these 1954 diaries describe are the life of a typical twelve year-old boy who's more interested in making model aeroplanes than producing any startling revelations about what he was doing at the BBC all day.

You did say Billie Gibson was a dish.
It's odd that Billie played the same parts that Hédi would be performing thirteen years later. They were quite different types of girl you know. Hédi was a natural intellectual: bright, incredibly well read, sophisticated but not in an actressy sort of way: she was at heart I think a very down to earth girl, no side, nothing pompous or affected about her at all.

That's certainly my reading of Hédi's character,

but come on, tell me about Billie! What was she like?

Young, brunette, vivacious, about twenty-five years old. You might have heard about British pantomime?

Christmas fairy stories with pop songs, cross-dressing and smut?

I'm impressed! The leading boy is always played by a pulchritudinous young girl with a loud singing voice and fat thighs, which she likes to slap vigorously at every conceivable opportunity. Billie Gibson would have made an ideal Dick Whittington. She had an open-air artlessness about her, she was friendly, direct and uncomplicated. Do you recognise the kind of girl I'm describing?

In the States we call girls like these cheerleaders. She doesn't exactly sound your type.

At the tender age of twelve, Billie Gibson was very definitely my type. I adored her. She immediately took a fancy to her young co-star and would sit next to me at rehearsals, her gorgeous thighs encased in what used to be called 'pedal pushers'– you know those clinging slacks cut short at the ankle?

They're back in fashion, Robin.

Fantastic. Anyway, sharing a script together, her thigh glued to mine and her arm draped around my shoulder, she would joke and snuggle up to me and I thought I was in heaven.

You obviously hadn't much previous sexual experience?

I hadn't reached puberty and I had absolutely no sexual experience. I'm ashamed to say that at twelve years old I didn't know what sex was. I knew nothing about the facts of life. My parents were too embarrassed to tell me and my school was too arty-farty and precious for there to be some fat kid with glasses who would explain everything to me behind the bike sheds. I know it sounds unbelievable but this was the 1950s!

So what did you do about Billie?

I didn't know what to do. I realised I couldn't become her boyfriend, she was a mature woman and I was a snotty-nosed kid. I was happy merely to be with her and I loved it when we had scenes in the serial to play together. Patrick Keith, our director must have realised that my performance went up several notches when I was acting with her because he was always very complimentary about my work with Billie.

He could tell there was some electricity there?

Everyone could. I suppose we were a bit of a joke on the set but no one minded because of the excellent performances. No one that is with the exception of Anna Lombard who was insanely jealous.

She liked you too?

She couldn't stand me but didn't like the idea that someone else could take a shine to me.

So how did this romance end up?
I'm sorry, I'm being very rude, you must be absolutely parched with all this talking. How about a
cup of coffee?

**I see, I'm not to know just yet but you are going
to tell me aren't you? I'd prefer a cup of tea if you
don't mind.**
I'll pop the kettle on and you can catch up with
your HK on Adrian Mackinder's masterpiece.

CHAPTER THREE
The Ghosts of Time!

Susan sat up in bed, rubbed her eyes and
stared out of the bedroom window. It was a beautiful summer's morning. Birds were singing loudly
in the sycamore trees that bordered the gravel
drive and beyond them the blue sea glinted invitingly in the distance. But she had awoken feeling
in some strange way very slightly disappointed. In
the rose garden below she could see but not hear
the water splashing about the Fountain of Time's
two white marble figures.

When Old Daniel had described the Fountains of Time to Michael and Susan as they travelled from the railway station to Monckton Manor
in the pony and trap, somehow in Susan's imagin-

ation she had pictured the fountain to be a very grand and important structure rather like those she had seen in Trafalgar Square. Or at least like the huge drinking fountain in the park at the end of Granny Summerwood's garden where you could climb up steps to an enormous black granite bowl and there were zinc cups on chains which could be held under half a dozen spurting jets of water.

As she looked down into the rose garden from her bedroom window, Susan observed a very matter-of-fact fountain indeed! The statues of the man and woman were no bigger than life-sized figures and from their lips and hands thin streams of water spurted into scallop shells at their feet. They stood in a raised pond which was perhaps twenty feet across but contained water not much more than a few inches deep. The figures were not the bronzed visages of great warriors or kings like those she had seen in the pages of encyclopaedias but of faces not much larger than Susan's own and the whole fountain with its three foot high surrounding wall hardly stood above the trellised roses strung along the side of the house. It had been too dark to see the fountain the previous evening but Uncle Philip had promised to take them round the rose garden this morning and tell the children the history of Monckton Manor and of the people who had lived in the house during the previous four hundred years.

"And will you tell us about the ghosts

and haunted rooms and galleries of Monckton Manor?" Susan had asked her Uncle excitedly after dinner.

"Ghosts? What ghosts?" Uncle Philip had laughed. "I've lived in this house since I was born and I never once heard of anyone in Monckton Manor ever seeing a ghost!"

"But there must be ghosts here," Susan had cried, "all old houses have ghosts!"

"Not this one, I'm afraid," said Aunt Julia firmly, "I know I wouldn't be able to stay a single second in a house with a ghost and even living in Kenya where you find all sorts of magic, witchcraft and mumbo-jumbo, neither your Uncle nor I ever saw anything the slightest bit ghost-like."

"Perhaps there were ghosts here but people were too frightened to say anything about them," said Michael helpfully as he saw the look of disappointment on Susan's face. "After all not everyone would want their friends to know that they live in a haunted house."

"I wouldn't mind!" muttered Uncle Philip.

"You can't mean that," said a shocked Aunt Julie. "What a thing to say in front of the children!"

"But it's true, Julie! If I could acquire the services of a nice friendly ghost I could open up the house to visitors at a shilling a head and all our money worries would be solved!"

Susan noticed that Aunt Julie had frowned at the mention of 'money worries' and wondered if Uncle Philip could really be as hard up as her parents had hinted when they had implored their children before they left for Monckton Manor not to ask for any expensive 'treats' from their hosts. No treats, and now no ghoulies or phantoms either! Uncle Philip and Aunt Julie had shown themselves to be kind hosts but as Susan climbed out of bed to get dressed she wondered just what sort of a holiday she and Michael had been let in for. If the next two or three weeks could be made to pass quickly then it looked as if the two children were going to have to make their own fun!

As promised, after breakfast, Uncle Philip took Michael and Susan to the rose garden to look at the Fountains of Time. Uncle Philip produced a large black key that he used to open the rusty iron lock on the door set in the high wall that abutted the east wing of Monckton Manor. Michael looked puzzled and asked his Uncle why such a high stone wall with such a thick wooden door would be needed to guard a few rose bushes.

"When Monckton Manor was a monastery this wasn't a rose garden but a kitchen garden, a sort of allotment where the monks would grow all their own fruit and vegetables. They needed such a heavy door and high wall to protect their main source of food. These days the walls are not there to guard the gardens from thieves, Michael," said Uncle Philip, "the roses themselves aren't really so valuable, it's to shelter the garden from the cold sea winds and also to provide a suntrap so that people can sit and enjoy the gardens on breezy days."

"And to keep the fountain jets from blowing all over the paving stones," added Susan and she ran to the walled rim of the fountain and splashed her hand in the water. The fountain actually looked much bigger than she had first supposed when she'd glanced down at it so disdainfully from her bedroom window this morning and she felt a sudden shiver of excitement as she looked at the two stern faces of the marble statues that stood in the centre of the fountain.

The figures were mounted on slabs of black granite which were arranged just beneath the water, the man gazing at the woman but the woman staring into the distance. Both had short curly hair and wide sensuous lips from which spouted a continuous stream of clear icy water that fell into scallop shells at their feet.

"The fountains in Trafalgar Square are driven by electric pumps," explained Uncle Philip, "and if there is ever a power cut then those fountains will stop working; but here the fountains are sited above a natural spring which runs down to the sea and it is said that the monks who toiled in this garden before Henry VIII disbanded the monastery in the Sixteenth Century all lived to a great age by drinking the waters."

"Old Daniel said that even before the

monks came here there was a fountain," said Michael taking a picture with his camera of the blank inscrutable faces of the marble figures.

"Indeed there was!" replied Uncle Philip. "Parish records which go back to the Middle Ages mention the Fountains of Time and there is good evidence to believe that they existed even in Roman days."

"Gosh, then they could be nearly two thousand years old!" exclaimed Susan.

"They could even be older than that," said Uncle Philip. "There have been excavations in this area which revealed the presence of Bronze-age and even Stone-age habitations. Some people say that the Fountains go back to the dawn of Time itself!"

"But they don't look that old," said Michael splashing the cold marble statues indignantly with his hand. "Stone-age men couldn't carve heads with fine detail like this surely?"

"You're absolutely right, of course, Michael. While the spring has probably always been here, the stone fountain itself must have been remade many times. This present one for instance dates from the middle of the Seventeen Century, probably about 1660, the time of Samuel Peyps and The Great Fire of London. You can tell by the carving of the writing beneath the stone heads."

Under the neck below each face like a necklace was a single ornately written word: beneath the man's face it said, 'Time', and beneath the woman's face it said 'Everlasting'.

"But what do those words mean?" said Susan with a very puzzled look on her face.

"You must come around to the other side of the fountain and read the poem inscribed on the plinth there," said Uncle Philip, "but I'm not sure that things will be made very much clearer for you."

The children went to the other side of the fountain and stared at the ornate writing on the marble plinth:

'Times Treasure lies about these Timeless Stones
For Those who take the Waters Twixt Times Bones
Times Treasure Here for Readers of this Rhyme
Time Everlasting for the Ghosts of Time'

"Treasure!" cried Michael excitedly.

"Quite a large treasure if village folk tales are to be believed," said Uncle Philip. "A few hours before Henry VIII's soldiers came to ransack the monastery during the Reformation some four hundred years ago, the Abbot was tipped off by a mysterious brother and sister who arrived on horseback at the monastery's doors during a thunderstorm and urged the monks to hide their gold plate and jewels before it could be plundered by Henry's troops."

"Who were they?" asked Susan.

"Now that's a great mystery, no one seems to know. Some say they were the son and daughter of a great noble family sympathetic to the old Roman Church, others say that they were spies in Henry VIII's pay and all too ready to trick the monks into handing over their wealth. But whoever they were the abbot believed their warning and more importantly he believed in them and he entrusted the young man and woman with the whole of the monastery's treasure so that they could secretly hide it whereby none of the monks would ever be able to reveal its whereabouts even under torture."

"But surely this brother and sister could have pretended to hide the treasure then just kept it for themselves?" said Michael.

"The legend says that the brother and sister did safely hide the treasure but that they were discovered by a vengeful mob of soldiers on their way home and set upon and brutally murdered before they could reveal the whereabouts of their hiding place."

"Gosh, how exciting!" said Susan. "But how did the poem come to be written?"

"That I'm afraid, no one really knows. Perhaps either the brother or sister was able to make a dying confession to one of the monks but we can't be sure. All that is certain in that the Fountains of Time became associated with the poem and it's been here ever since."

"But the rhyme doesn't make sense," said Michael disappointedly.

"You're not the first person to have said that!" laughed Uncle Philip, "Perhaps your sister will find the answer to the riddle."

Susan was busy copying the words into her pocket diary. Clearly the poem would need to be studied very carefully if the meaning was to be revealed. The Ghosts of Time! How thrilling that for a resolutely unhaunted house the word 'Ghosts' should suddenly appear like this, and in the rose garden of all places!

"Do we know who the carved faces are supposed to be?" asked Michael.

"Some say the male is the Roman God Janus, who was the god of gates and doors in Roman mythology. Janus is supposed to represent new beginnings – one must pass through a gate or door before entering a new place." said Uncle Philip, "It's where we get the name for our month, January: one face looking back to the old year and one looking forward to the new. But of course Janus would have been a male god, the faces here are quite obviously male and female."

Susan finished writing the poem and stepped up to the fountain's wall and stared hard into the impassive stone faces. "The man is Time, so he looks back into the past and the woman is Everlasting, so she belongs to the future. The Fountains of Time should have a third figure to represent the present."

"I never heard that the fountains ever had a third statue." Said Uncle Philip. Now if you two would like to go for a swim in the bay before lunch I suggest you get started. It's going to be a hot day and you won't want to rush back."

Steeple Bay was half a mile from Monckton Manor and so the children lost no time in fetching bathing costumes from their bedrooms and setting off along the leafy winding lane that led down to the sea. Uncle Philip was right, it was a very warm day indeed and by the time Michael and Susan finally clambered down a steep path in the cliff onto the beach they both felt hot and sticky and dying for a lovely bathe.

The sea was surprisingly cold but very refreshing and after their swim brother and sister lay on towels and discussed what they wanted to do during the next two or three weeks of their holiday.

"It would be lovely if we could solve the Fountain's riddle and actually see the Ghosts of Time," said Susan.

"I'm not sure I actually want to see any ghosts, thanks very much," frowned Michael. "I'm much more interested in finding the treasure. It would be wonderful if we could discover a great oak chest full of gold chalices, plates and precious jewels and present it to Uncle Philip and Aunt Julie and say, 'You don't need to scrimp and save anymore, you can do Monckton Manor up from top to bottom then charge visitors a shilling a time to wander around the house and gardens'"

"But people have been looking for the missing treasure for absolutely ages, Michael. Uncle Philip told us that over a hundred years ago they even excavated beneath the fountain, right down to the natural spring and they found precisely nothing."

"Perhaps they weren't looking in the right place. I'm sure the treasure has remained hidden because no one has managed to solve the mystery of the poem carved on the wall," said Michael reasonably.

"That's because it doesn't make any sense," Susan frowned. "If clever people like Uncle Philip have been trying to explain the riddle for the last three hundred years what makes you think a couple of kids like us are going to crack it?"

"Well, we can try can't we, have you got your diary with you? Let's have another look at the verse."

Susan took her diary from her jacket pocket and flicked through the pages.

"Here we are, Michael:

'Times Treasure lies about these Timeless Stones

For Those who take the Waters Twixt Times Bones

Times Treasure Here for Readers of this

Rhyme
    Time Everlasting for the Ghosts of Time'

Her brother scratched his head and looked very puzzled. "It doesn't make any sense at all when you read it quickly like that. Perhaps it would be best if we took just one line at a time and you read it very slowly."

"Times........ trea-...........sure .... lies...."

"Not that slowly, you idiot!"

Susan giggled and read out the line properly:

"Times Treasure lies about these Timeless Stones."

She frowned for a second and then her face brightened. "That's easy to understand: the treasure is lying about somewhere, perhaps beneath the paving stones which make up the pathways in the rose garden."

        "Then why hasn't anyone found it?" enquired Michael. "Uncle Philip told us that not only has the fountain itself been excavated but all the paving stones in the rose garden have been taken up and dug under at one time or another. No, we've got to think much harder about the poem than simply taking all the words at face value. For instance, "Times Treasure lies about these Timeless Stones", we think the treasure lies beneath something but perhaps the word 'lies' means not to tell the truth: in other words the treasure is no-where near the fountain or the rose garden!"

Susan bit her lip and frowned again. "But if the verse is talking of lies in the first three words how can we believe anything the rest of the poem tells us?"

"I don't know but let's have a look at the second line, what does it say?"

"For Those who take the Waters Twixt Times Bones"

We have to carry the water somewhere?" asked Susan helpfully.

"No, the word 'take' doesn't mean literally to carry the water. When you take the waters at a spa like Bath or Baden-Baden you just drink it or bathe in it – you don't actually carry the stuff any-where, it's just an expression. But what on earth are "Times Bones"?"

"Dead bodies! Ghosts!"

"You might be right, Susan, ghosts are cer-tainly mentioned later on."

"What does 'twixt' mean, Michael?"

"It's short for 'betwixt' an old way of saying 'between'."

Susan pulled a face: "Why would anyone want to drink or bathe in water between someone's bones? It doesn't make sense and even if it did it sounds perfectly horrible."

"At least the third line of the poem seems straightforward enough:

"Times Treasure Here for Readers of this Rhyme"

"If we can solve the riddle the treasure will be ours."

"Yes," said Susan, "that's easy, but what about the last line:

'Time Everlasting for the Ghosts of Time?"'

"It means that if we can solve the riddle of the rhyme then not only will the treasure be ours but also the Ghosts of Time will find Time everlasting – in other words the ghosts will be able to rest in peace after their long vigil."

"But who are the Ghosts of Time, Michael?"

"The guardians of the treasure I suppose," said Michael. "The brother and sister who hid the treasure before being killed by Henry VIII's soldiers, or a couple of ancient ghostly monks unable to rest until the treasure is restored to its rightful owners."

"But who are the rightful owners? The monks of Henry VIII's time have all been dead for centuries and the monastery has long since disappeared."

"Since Uncle Philip now owns Monckton Manor I think he and Aunt Julie should get the treasure, after all he is the vicar of Monckton village so I suppose you could say he was a sort of modern-day monk."

"Yes, it would be lovely to surprise Uncle

Philip and Aunt Julie," said Susan, her eyes shining, "and all we have to do is solve the riddle and dig the treasure up!"

Michael laughed, "Somehow Susan, I don't think finding the treasure is going to be quite as simple as that!"

FOUR

You've told me how you loved going to the BBC and playing Michael in the serial but how did the rest of the cast feel about appearing in 'The Fountains of Time'?

What do you mean, 'How did they feel'?

Did they hate acting on kids' TV in this farrago of nonsensical bullshit?

Quite the opposite, Jennifer, and I blush at your obviously low opinion of Adrian Mackinder's beautiful book, which you haven't found time to read. Unlike some actors today who seem more interested in presenting the public with their self-image rather than providing paying customers with some sort of interesting entertainment, in 1954 the cast of 'The Fountains of Time' were positively delighted and honoured to be appearing on children's television on a Sunday evening and did their very best to present the serial as finely as possible. They certainly didn't look down on the project as if it was somehow beneath them.

I apologise, I didn't mean to –

Not at all, Jenny, you're from the States and your ignorance of show business in 1950's Britain is perfectly understandable, after all isn't that why you are interviewing me? We all loved acting in the serial, even the appalling Anna Lombard. Mind you, it is true that in those days the BBC paid terrible money.

How much did they pay you?
Twelve guineas, that's about fifty American dollars an episode.

Jeez, is that all?
The adult members of the cast obviously got more. The entire budget of the serial would have only been about £3000. The BBC didn't pay actors a fortune but it was perhaps two or three times more than we'd have earned in Rep. It was ten weeks paid work and I can tell you that in postwar austerity Britain we were all bloody grateful to get it.

There were no prima donnas in the cast then?
Apart, as I have said, from Anna Lombard who thought she was a cut above everybody else, but nobody took any notice of her, or her mother. No, we were a very happy team. I was twelve years old in my first big part on television and intensely enthusiastic and impressionable and I absolutely adored the cast, the camera crew, the soundmen, the technicians, the director – marvellous, marvellous people.

You adored Billie Gibson!
I did too! It was the first time that I fell in love with anyone and it hit me bloody hard, I can tell you.

She was in her twenties and you were twelve years old, what on earth did you think you were going to do about it?
I quickly decided that I wanted to spend the rest of my life with gorgeous Billie and that as soon as I reached the age of sixteen I would ask her to marry me.

You did get it bad!
I was a callow, extremely romantic teenager and very ripe for love. It seems I grew up and entered the adult world almost overnight. My homework suffered – what could Henry V mean to a boy in love? I no longer liked to listen to comedy shows on the radio and my beautiful Keil Kraft turbo-prop lay unfinished on the kitchen table, much to my father's annoyance. But there was no helping me: I had eyes only for La Gibson.

The minx must have encouraged you!
I think so. She was very familiar with me, very tactile, always putting her arm around my shoulder and hugging me at every opportunity. She liked to fool around with me when she thought no one was looking – goose my bottom, that sort of thing.

Shit, Robin, she wanted locking up!

No one knew what the word paedophilia meant in
those days of course and it was certainly not the
norm for young women to touch up young boys.
But I'm probably being terribly unfair to Billie; I
think she was just a very affectionate girl who occasionally let things get a bit out of hand. I was so
very inexperienced with women and had no idea
of how to play the game of love. She must have
thought I was extremely naïve and childish and
I'm quite certain had no inkling what I felt about
her.

Didn't you speak to Billie about your feelings?

Gawd no! Apart from when I was acting, I was
a very shy child remember; but I did concoct
this ingenious but utterly hare-brained scheme
whereby Miss Gibson would come and live with
me and my family in our little terraced house in
Sydenham.

**How did that work out? I'm sorry, Robin, I really
shouldn't laugh!**

Actually, Jennifer, my scheme could have been a
goer. Billie was very much a peripatetic sort of actress who never seemed to stay in one place for
more than five minutes – always being turned out
of boarding houses, YWCAs, for various reasons
not unconnected with her never having earned
enough money to pay the rent. Although looking
back now there was probably a good deal of 'man

trouble' as well. I thought a nice homely pied-a-terre in South London, a twenty-minute train ride to the West End, would be ideal for her; she'd muck in with my mum and sisters and I would be able to see my adored one every day. When the four years were up we could get married and find a place of our own. I'd have been sixteen and she'd have been knocking thirty. Bleedin' ridiculous wasn't it?

I'm twenty-eight and I couldn't begin to imagine ever marrying a teenage boy!
Don't give up, Jennifer, there's still time! I did tell you I was a good-looking young fellow, didn't I?

Let's read some more of your diary!
Fine, but we'll skip forward a bit if you don't mind, there's an awful lot of boring repetition that will put you into a coma.

Monday, 25th October, 1954

Cold and frosty. Breakfast: porridge – yuk!! No HK this week as massive amount of lines to learn for episode 3.

Ilovebilliegibsonilovebilliegibsonilovebilliegibsonilovebilliegibsonilovebilliegibsonilovebilliegibsonilovebilliegibsonilovebilliegibsonilovebilliegibsonilovebilliegibsonilovebilliegibson.

Lawrence showed me incredible trick with 2

packs of playing cards and a piece of cotton. Missing card rises from pack using cotton up sleeve .... FANTASTIC!!!!!

Excuse me for interrupting; along with Miss Gibson, you also loved the old guy who played Daniel. There was a definite empathy between you?
Like me, Lawrence England had been a child actor, but in Queen Victoria's reign. He knew every wrinkle in the business and was an absolute fund of theatrical stories. I suppose he'd be considered a stultifying old bore by young actors these days but in the 1950s there was no better way for young pros to understand the nuts and bolts of show business. Drama school taught me a lot about dancing and music and acting technique but it was Lawrence who taught me how to cope with the day-to-day rigours of being a professional actor. He'd done the lot: silent films; Shakespeare at Stratford; music-hall and variety; adverts for Radio Luxembourg; magic shows on television in the Thirties at Ally Pally; he'd played before Queen Mary at Windsor and sung outside Kensington tube station in the rain for pennies.

I can understand why you took to the old boy, but wasn't he just an ancient theatrical queen lusting after your body?
Certainly not! He was probably the age then that I am now. I hope people don't think I'm an old

queen because I take a paternal interest in the young actors I work with. Lawrence was a bit strange and eccentric but he was a nice man. If he made mistakes in his life – as we all do – and if one or two of these mistakes were to rebound on me then I forgave him a long time ago, and I forgive him all over again now.

OK, Robin. Back to the diary again!
We'll shoot forward to the week of Episode four, which I think you'll find quite interesting.

Wednesday, 3rd November, 1954.

BG held my hand under the table at lunch and I thought I was going to die!!!!!!! If I can only find out where the treasure is then we can be together for always and everything will be all right for us!!

Thursday, 4th November.

The Programme Controller came to watch us re-hearse and picked me out for special praise. He said that I was 'Unbelievably believable' – think I know what he meant. But I was good!!!! The clues are coming thick and fast now! Will I discover the treasure before the end of the serial????? Billie wore pale blue knitted polo neck jumper.......very tight!! She is unbelievably believable!!!!!!!!!!!!!!

Treasure? What's this about?

The gold plate and jewels Henry VIII stole from the monks in Adrian Mackinder's novel. By the time we'd begun rehearsing episode four I'd come to believe that the treasure in the story actually existed and that by the end of the serial I would have discovered its whereabouts.

Robin?
It sounds quite extraordinary but I had become so engrossed in playing my role that I'd begun to assume that I really was Michael Summerwood and that by the end of episode six I would find the lost treasure just as the children do in the book.

You're not serious?
It does seem extremely odd to me even now but at the end of the serial I put it down to a mild delusion – like believing in Santa Claus or the tooth fairy. I'd not had such a large role to play in anything before and certainly I'd never identified with a part so completely. It hasn't happened to me since, but by the time we came to rehearse the fourth episode of the serial I was beginning to seriously delude myself into believing that Michael Summerwood was a real person and that I had somehow become him. The logic of this impossibility seemed to have escaped me, again like supposedly sensible children believing that a corpulent Father Christmas can squeeze down a two-foot wide chimney with a bag full of presents without covering himself from head to toe in soot. The cardboard sets in the studio suddenly

became real, the props I handled were real Jaco-
bean daggers and real loaded pistols; my fellow
actors had also morphed into the actual characters they were playing.

**But that's ridiculous, you couldn't possibly be-
lieve 'The Fountains of Time' had become true,
you could see all the cameras and microphone
booms and things.**
I persuaded myself that the whole production was
a sort of giant red-herring, a device for believing
that the treasure didn't exist: it was only a made-
up story, when all the time I knew it was a conspir-
acy to hide the truth. I would find the treasure by
episode six and move my parents and sisters and
lover to a nice house by the sea in Devon where I'd
live forever more in peace and happiness with the
delectable Billie Gibson.

People must have thought you were crazy!
I was quite sneaky and wasn't caught very often. I
do remember once being alone on the set of Beau
Brummel's parlour when everyone had broken for
lunch with a screwdriver in my hand taking out
the pieces of hardboard in the oak panelling in
order to get at what I believed to be the secret
cache. I was screwing them back when a stagehand
suddenly appeared and asked me what I was playing at.

And what did you say?
I told him I was testing out my new screwdriver,

and he wandered off shaking his head.

Where did you think such a treasure could come from?

Remember I had read 'The Fountains of Time' before I acted in the serial so I was quite aware that Michael and Susan do find the treasure at the end of the story and so I was quite confident that by the time the production finished the booty would be mine. I suppose at the back of my mind I must have believed that Adrian Mackinder was responsible for laying the treasure trail. I knew he liked me and he was perfectly aware that I came from a modest background. For all I knew he was a millionaire author amusing himself with a treasure hunt as a roundabout way of giving me a start in life.

It sounds like the plot of 'Great Expectations'.

Yes, doesn't it? That of course was another book I'd devoured and loved. I may have been a very naïve twelve-year old but I really did believe that fortunes could come to adventurous young boys from undisclosed benefactors.

You must have been quite mad. Had you become ill with overwork?

Not at all, I was deluded into believing something that wasn't true. I wasn't ill in any way, in fact I felt great, and I certainly wasn't mad! I behaved quite normally: mixed with the cast as usual, learnt my lines, acted the part of Michael; only I

didn't believe I was acting anymore. My performance benefited enormously: I became the person
of Michael Summerwood. I really was looking for
that bloody treasure!

31. INT. SUSAN'S BEDROOM. STUDIO. NIGHT

(IT IS MIDNIGHT AND A THUNDERSTORM IS
FLASHING AND RUMBLING IN THE DISTANCE AS
MICHAEL IN PYJAMAS AND BARE FEET RUSHES
ACROSS TO HIS SISTER'S BED AND BEGINS TO
SHAKE HER AWAKE)

MICHAEL: Susan, wake up! You must wake up!

SUSAN: (VERY SLEEPILY) Go back to bed, Michael,
I'm fast asleep.

MICHAEL: But you've got to wake up, Susan, I've
discovered the meaning of the rhyme!

SUSAN: What did you say?

MICHAEL: The poem of The Fountains of Time,
I've discovered what it means. You were right all
along, Susan, we must go to the rose garden now!

SUSAN: But it's the middle of the night, Michael
and I'm so tired, can't we go in the morning?

MICHAEL: Of course not! Don't you want to find
the treasure?

SUSAN: Not now, not at this moment, I want to go

back to sleep!

MICHAEL: Susan, if you don't get out of bed and come with me this instant, I shall go down to the garden and discover the treasure all by myself!

SUSAN: (WAKING UP RAPIDLY AND RUBBING HER EYES) But you can't have found out what the poem means. People have been studying it for hundreds of years and no one's managed to understand neither head nor tail of it.

MICHAEL: I have, Susan! I've just had the most incredible dream where the Spirits of the Fountain appeared to me and said that the Summerwood children have been chosen to find the treasure but we have to begin looking straight away. Don't you see that if we leave it until the morning we might miss our start!

SUSAN: Gosh, Michael how exciting! Do you think we should wake up Uncle Philip and Aunt Julie to tell them where we're going?

MICHAEL: Of course not! The Spirits told me that the Summerwood children alone would discover the whereabouts of the treasure; not the Summerwood children, Uncle Philip and Aunt Julie, Old Daniel and half the rest of the village of Monckton. Do buck up, Susan and get your dressing gown, there can only be a few hours of darkness before it gets light and then it will be too late!

SUSAN: I'm coming, Michael! I'm coming!

32. EXT. THE ROSE GARDEN'S FOUNTAIN. STUDIO. NIGHT

(IT IS NOT ACTUALLY RAINING BUT THE THUNDER AND LIGHTENING IS GETTING CLOSER WITH STEADY FLASHES ILLUMINATING THE FOUNTAINS)

MICHAEL: (APPROACHING) Do hurry up, Susan!

SUSAN: What's all the rush is about?

MICHAEL: I can't get this fantastic dream out of my mind where the faces on the fountain came alive and told me to go immediately to the rose garden, and when I woke up I suddenly realised that I had solved the riddle of the poem.

SUSAN: But why should we have been chosen by the Spirits to find the treasure rather than someone else?

MICHAEL: I haven't the faintest idea. The Fountain Faces said, that the Summerwood children would eventually discover the treasure because Susan Summerwood had solved the riddle of the rhyme.

SUSAN: Me? I don't remember solving anything.

MICHAEL: But you did, Susan! Don't you remember the first two lines of the verse:

'Times treasure lies about these timeless stones

  For those who take the waters twixt Times bones.'

You thought to 'take the waters' meant you actually had to carry it and I said that you were mistaken and that it really meant to drink or bathe in it. But what if you're right? Suppose we do have to carry the fountain's water to some place!

SUSAN: But to where, Michael?

MICHAEL: It's simple: we have to take the 'waters twixt Times bones'.

SUSAN: I'm sorry, I still don't understand.

MICHAEL: Don't you remember how odd we thought it was for the fountain's cups to be made into the shape of seashells?

SUSAN: Yes, I do but –

MICHAEL: Can't you see, Susan? Scallop shells are like the shellfish's bones only outside instead of inside, like our skeletons.

SUSAN: Gosh, Michael!

MICHAEL: For those who take the waters twixt Time's bones, means we have to take the water from shell to shell. You see you were right all the time!

SUSAN: Oh, Michael, you are clever! Let's do it now, have you anything to carry the water in?

MICHAEL: (PRODUCING PAPER CUPS FROM PYJAMA POCKET) Cups from the picnic hamper! But we must do this properly. (MICHAEL CLIMBS INTO THE FOUNTAIN'S BOWL AND HELPS HIS SISTER UP. THEY SPLASH IN THE SHALLOW WATER UNTIL THEY'RE STANDING BENEATH THE STATUES) You stand by the woman's face –

SUSAN: 'EVERLASTING'.

MICHAEL: That's right; and I'll stand by 'TIME', the man's face. We'll each dip our cups into the water of our shells then pass the cups to each other and empty them into the shells and see what happens.

SUSAN: Golly, how exciting!

MICHAEL: Ready, Susan?

SUSAN: Pass me your cup – here's mine.

(THEY EXCHANGE CUPS THEN LOOK AT EACH OTHER EXPECTANTLY)

MICHAEL: Right, on the count of three empty the cups into the shells.

SUSAN: Oh, can I count — please?

MICHAEL: Yes, all right but do it really slowly.

SUSAN: Very well. One ... Two ... Three!

(THE CHILDREN EMPTY THEIR CUPS INTO THE FOUNTAIN'S SHELLS AND STAND FOR A LONG TIME FROZEN WITH EXPECTATION. SUSAN IS THE FIRST TO EXPRESS HER DISAPPOINTMENT THAT NOTHING HAS HAPPENED)

MICHAEL: Let's try it again.

(THE CHILDREN FILL AND EMPTY THEIR CUPS INTO THE FOUNTAIN'S SHELLS FOR A SECOND TIME BUT WITH THE SAME RESULT)

SUSAN: Oh Michael, what a swizzle!

(THEY BOTH WADE BACK TO THE PERIMETER OF THE BOWL, CLIMB DOWN AND SLUMP DEJECT- EDLY AGAINST THE BASE OF THE FOUNTAIN)

MICHAEL: Well, I suppose it was worth a try.

SUSAN: It was a jolly good idea, Michael.

MICHAEL: I expect I got part of it wrong. Perhaps you have to say the rhyme or something.

SUSAN: I'll say it now! (SHE CLOSES HER EYES AND RECITES THE POEM FROM MEMORY VERY SLOWLY AND QUIETLY)

'Times treasure lies about these timeless stones
For those who take the waters twixt Times bones

Times treasure here for readers of this rhyme

Time everlasting for the Ghosts of Time'

(THERE IS A GREAT FLASH OF LIGHTENING FOLLOWED IMMEDIATELY BY A HUGE CLAP OF THUNDER AND IT BEGINS TO RAIN HARD. MICHAEL AND SUSAN CLASP EACH OTHER IN TERROR AND WE BEGIN TO CLOSE INTO THEIR FACES)

MICHAEL: (POINTING ALONG ONE OF THE ROSE GARDEN'S STONE PATHS) Look, Susan, look!

33. EXT.THE ROSE GARDEN PATH TOWARDS THE DOOR IN THE WALL. STUDIO. NIGHT

(TWO DIFFUSE FIGURES OF LIGHT APPEAR THROUGH THE DOOR AND BEGIN TO MOVE SLOWLY ALONG THE PATH TOWARDS THE CHIL-DREN)

34. EXT. THE ROSE GARDEN'S FOUNTAIN. STU-DIO. NIGHT

(CLOSE UP TIGHT ON CHILDREN'S EXCITED RAIN-SOAKED FACES)

SUSAN: Ghosts!

MICHAEL: The Ghosts of Time!

GRAMS: CLOSING MUSIC

Billie Gibson making her big entrance in the serial as a diffuse figure!

Yes, anxious fathers sitting with their children at home would have to wait for next week's thrilling instalment before they could clap their eyes on the gorgeous star of our show! Actually you can see her now in this marvellous advert that her slavering co-star clipped and treasured from 'Woman's Weekly':

Lovely Billie Gibson, star of

B.B.C. Television's new Sunday Serial, "The Fountains of Time"

always uses **Smith's Cremolia Skin Cream** to keep her hands looking soft and smooth.

Billie says,

"Regular use of **Smith's Cremolia Skin Cream** protects my skin from the heat of studio lights and also keeps my hands from flaking and chapping in the wintry weather – try a jar yourself and see!"

Available from any branch of Boots the Chemist 1/2d & 2/1d

OK, Robin, so we have two on-going elements powerfully influencing your appearances in the 1954 production of 'The Fountains of Time': firstly, you are deluded into believing that somehow you have become the character of Michael Summerwood and you are actively seeking to find a treasure which couldn't possibly exist. Secondly, you are madly in love with Billie Gibson, an older and absolutely unsuitable woman for a boy of your tender years, and you've concocted a crazy scheme to win her affections. So how does it all end up?

Do you know something, Jennifer, I'm astounded that you're the slightest bit interested. None of this has anything whatever to do with the book about Hédi Gela you're supposed to be writing.

You are a bloody tease, Robin. Fine, so when I've finished Hédi Gela's biography I'll write a book about you. How's that?

Don't think you'd sell many copies.

I'm not so sure, you certainly know how to make a girl wonder.

First of all you must understand that my delusions about finding the treasure and my love for Billie Gibson – I think we can call love a delusion, can't we? – were completely compartmentalised. They were quite separate parts of my life and although it must appear that on occasions they would get in each other's way and upset each other's hold over my power of belief, this never actually happened. When Billie was playing a character in the story with me my love for the actress was moment-arily suppressed and I functioned completely as Michael Summerwood. When I was with her in the canteen at lunchtime it was then that the treasure seeking delusion receded into the background and my feelings of love for Billie became uppermost.

Crazy mixed-up kid! So how did things resolve themselves?
In an extremely dramatic and very unpleasant fashion, I'm afraid. My diary is apparently too shocked to tell you about it.

Tuesday, 9th November, 1954.

Disaster.

Wednesday, 10th November, 1954.

Hateful day.

Thursday, 11th November, 1954.

A cold horrible day. I'm so sick of this work I wish I was back at school. I hate BG so much I wish she was dead.

Friday, 12th November, 1954.

Transmission of Episode 5. I was quite good but I despise myself. Can't wait till next week when this nightmare will all be over.

Saturday, 13th November, 1954.

Dad took me to see Charlton play Wolves at the Valley. Burst into tears at the end of the match. Dad thought it was because we had lost!

Jesus, Robin, what the hell happened to you?
I had finally plucked up the courage to tell Billie how I felt about her and had left a note in her message box asking if I could come and see her in her dressing room after a break in rehearsals. We both had an hour off on that Monday afternoon because we weren't needed in a couple of quite complicated rehearsal scenes in Studio G that required some considerable technical work. As a minor – though not a minor character — I was in a large communal dressing room with most of the cast. Billie, being a feature player had her own small dressing room hidden away in the depths of Lime Grove, you'd never find it if you didn't know where it was.

Oh my God, I think I know what's going to happen.
I don't think you do; but you're right in the impli-

cation that Billie did not receive my note and certainly wasn't expecting me to call at that time.

You barged in without knocking.
I did not barge in without knocking. I tapped po-
litely on the door and waited. A small voice said,
'Come in', so I opened the door and found Billie
standing there without a stitch on.

As I figured.
Lying on the floor in his underpants and as dead as
fish paste was Lawrence England.

Oh no!
Like myself he had been an occasional secret visitor to Billie's dressing room during the run of the
serial and unlike me he'd taken full advantage of
her juicy young body. He died as all old men would
wish to die: moving from paradise in this world to
paradise in the next in the space of a screw. Billie
didn't know what to do. I told her to get dressed
and began to look for Lawrence's clothes.

You were going to cover up what happened?
I discovered for the first time what has since become a most useful facet of my character: that I
am good in a crisis. I realised instinctively that I
had to get Lawrence dressed and his corpse out of
Billie's dressing room.

**Why would you want to do this, after her savage
betrayal of your affections – the bitch must have
known how you felt about her?**

I really don't think she did know. Anyway I did it for the sake of 'The Fountains of Time'. I was an old showbiz trouper even at twelve. What was the point of having all that scandal attached to the production? How would the truth have benefited anyone? I got the old boy dressed with the utmost difficulty, dragged him into the passage then raised the alarm.

What happened?
Nothing really. They called a doctor who pronounced him dead from a massive heart attack. He was carted out, by a little-used side entrance to a waiting ambulance and that was the last anyone saw of him. I don't think there was even an autopsy. Apparently he'd been to see his doctor about some minor complaint during the previous three weeks and the death certificate was signed on the basis that he was somewhat overweight and had been warned that his drinking and heavy smoking was endangering his health therefore there was no need for a post mortem.

So what did Billie have to say to you later?
What you'd expect: I wasn't to be too upset by what had taken place. Sex is too stupid for words, when I grew up I'd understand that people do the most ridiculous things. Their relationship wasn't meant to be serious – just a bit of fun — it was a one-off. I mustn't think badly of her because of a stupid bit of nonsense that didn't mean anything. Lawrence was like a father to her, she respected

him. They'd gone to the pub together at lunch-time and had a few too many. He'd become over-amorous and she'd felt sorry for the silly old sod and things got a bit out of hand, that's all. There was nothing premeditated about it, just Dame Mother Nature playing a daft trick on the pair of them. Lawrence actually conked out before any-thing really serious had happened – she claimed – and it was all best forgotten and she hoped that we could still be best friends.

Did you attend the funeral?
No one from the BBC went. Lawrence had a mar-ried daughter as his sole heir who disliked all as-pects of her father's rackety theatrical life and so he was cremated without his theatrical cronies and show biz pals even knowing where and when to raise a last glass to their old chum.

How did the BBC manage without Old Daniel in 'The Fountains of Time'?
Perfectly well, they simply hired another actor to play his part.

Didn't viewers notice the difference?
I don't think so. I never heard that anyone wrote in to the BBC to complain that one week, Old Daniel was played by Lawrence England and the follow-ing week he was played by someone else. Picture quality wasn't very high in those black and white days remember and the role required quite a lot of make-up: chop whiskers, that sort of thing.

Surely the newspapers of the time pounced on the story?

The British Press in those days very much looked down its nose at television and, not like today, was utterly uninterested in the BBC's goings on. For all the enthusiasm of the participants, telly programmes were somewhat hit and miss affairs. There were lots of breakdowns in transmission and cards would appear on the screen informing viewers that 'Normal Service will be resumed as soon as possible.' They'd sit obediently watching an interlude film of a kitten playing with a ball of wool for ten minutes until the fault was rectified. Nobody, including the Press, took television at all seriously.

So Lawrence England died unmourned and unremembered?

Didn't even get an obit. in 'The Stage', which is extraordinary when you think what the man had given to the business for nigh on sixty years. Still he did get to give Billie Gibson a poke, which is more than I ever did.

Does it still rankle after all these years?

Hmm, since you mention it, yes it does. If I could, I'd like to travel back in time like the children do in 'The Fountains of Time', suddenly appear in Billie Gibson's dressing room, pull down those ultra-tight pedal-pushers from her luscious plump thighs and give her a thoroughly good seeing-to.

You'd have a heart attack like poor old Lawrence.
Probably! Talking of obituaries, you won't have
seen poor Adrian Mackinder's from 'The Times',
which I kept because he was the first, and come
to think of it, probably the last really great man I
ever met.

The Times, 10th April, 1966

Adrian Mackinder, who died on April 5, 1966 at the age
of 87 at his home in Kingsbridge, South Devon, made a modest but distinctive contribution to children's literature in this
century.

His public esteem fluctuated considerably during his long
life, from wide and affectionate recognition as a best selling
author of children's books to a last long period of neglect
when few of his successes were left in print and only the die-
hard enthusiast remained to praise works of fantasy which
in the age of commercial television, graphic comics and horror films had come to be seen as somewhat sentimental and
dated.

Adrian Gordon Mackinder was born in 1879, the last of five
children by the Reverend John Mackinder and his wife Sarah
in the village of Tomich near Lairg. His love of literature came
from his mother who would read the works of Scott and Stevenson to him in the long dark winter evenings, supplement-
ing such stirring fare with tales of her own imagination and
instilling into him a life-long love of adventure stories.

On leaving school at the age of twelve he attempted nu-
merous employments with varying degrees of success until
finally he arrived at the news desk of 'The Glasgow Herald'
where, after a number of missed deadlines and consequent
altercations with the editor, he was demoted – or as he later
claimed, promoted – to the Children's Page. It was a short
step from editing material for publication to writing poems
and stories himself. Mackinder discovered the happy knack,
not so common among children's writers, of seeing the world

from a child's point of view and his stories soon began to appear in other publications including the 'Church Times' and 'Tiny Tim's Weekly'. A brief flirtation with 'The Magnet' was mutually ended when it was apparent that Mackinder could not keep up with the pace of composition demanded by an editor more accustomed to the prolificacy of Billy Bunter's famous creator, Frank Richards.

On the outbreak of war in 1914 Mackinder attempted to enlist with two of his brothers in the Royal Navy but he was rejected because of poor eyesight. In his somewhat selective autobiography, 'As I Remember', published in 1958, he claimed to have spent the war years travelling the Orient collecting folk tales for a prospective anthology, but no work of this description ever appeared and it was later rumoured that he travelled at the behest of the British Secret Service. At the war's end Mackinder entered a golden period of children's fiction and he contributed to many magazines and began to write a series of full-length historical novels for children including, 'The Captain of Cadiz' and 'Fortune's Castle' that quickly caught the attention of the more thoughtful and discerning child. It was in 1931 that one of his few works for adult readers was published, 'Night Things' a collection of extremely unpleasant ghost stories along the lines of M.R. James, that has become something of a collectors item for enthusiasts of the genre.

By the 1940s Mackinder had retired to South Devon where he composed his final works including 'The Madcap Pirates' and his best book, 'The Fountains of Time'. After initial poor reviews this last novel suddenly became popular as the result of a BBC Television adaptation in 1954 that sacrificed most of the religious and mystical elements for the fun and slapstick humour of a pair of time-travelling children. A heavily rumoured sequel to the novel was unforthcoming and although Mackinder seemed not to mind the neglect of his last years, the rare fan letter would always be answered in full by return of post usually accompanied by a signed photograph pictured with one of his favourite Scottish terriers. The author was unmarried.

Mackinder died here in Kingsbridge – was this his cottage?

Yes it was. The desk you see by the window is where he wrote 'The Fountains of Time'.

Gee, I didn't realise you were such a fan of the guy, and there was me being so rude about his writing. That's perfectly all right. Like fine wine Mackinder's works do not appear to travel well. He wouldn't have sold many copies of his books in the United States. I suppose his style wouldn't have the energy and crassness to appeal to American kids.

OK, I asked for that! Did you see Billie Gibson again? Yes, about fifteen years later. I switched the telly on for my kids one Saturday morning and discovered her presenting a live puppet show on ITV. Very good: nice interaction with the puppets and audience. She'd bring up these ghastly little brats in front of the cameras and was quite delightful with them. As you can imagine working with unrehearsed children would have been something of a challenge but she had the knack of making them do what she wanted in an entertaining way without having to bully or patronise them – it's a clever trick if you can pull it off.

Did she do anything else? She became quite popular as a result of the show: appeared on quiz programmes, panel games, that sort of thing. I think she even made principle boy in some seaside pantomime, so she did get a chance to slap those marvellous thighs. Died of cancer in the 1970s, and wasn't at all old — left a husband and two young children behind. Sad.

Now tell me about the end of the 1954 production of 'The Fountains of Time'. How did everything finish up?
We transmitted the final episode on the Sunday evening and I was back at school on Monday morning.

What happened about your delusion of really finding the 'Fountain's' treasure; did that evaporate with the shock of discovering Billie Gibson's infidelity and Lawrence England's dead body?
No, it stayed with me right until the camera's red light went out on the Sunday evening of that final episode, and then I was myself again.

Just like that?
Absolutely! But of course that is how I'd been programmed to react. I'm quite certain that although Lawrence England was responsible for hypnotising me he also left a command that I should return to normal at the end of the serial.

Robin! Lawrence England hypnotised you into believing you were Michael Summerwood and the treasure really existed and was waiting to be found?
I'm positive it was the old rogue. What happened was this: I'd got a note from my director, Patrick Keith, after the transmission of episode

three which contained one or two rather derogatory remarks about my performance. He said it had 'dipped'. My acting no longer seemed quite as credible as it had done in the first two episodes. I had become a bit self-conscious, my performance no longer had the 'ring of authenticity' about it. Perhaps I could get myself into a more receptive state of mind before I tackled rehearsals for episode four on the following Monday morning. Well of course I obviously couldn't handle being in love with Billie Gibson, and acting a strenuous role at the same time, it was all too much for a twelve-year old kid to take on. Naturally I confided the contents of Patrick's note to my newest bestest chum, Lawrence England, and as a result he must have decided, either out of devilment or as a joke — or because he honestly thought it would actually help, to surreptitiously hypnotise me into believing I was acting Michael Summerwood for real.

He must have learnt hypnotism as part of some stage act he'd got up at sometime. God, what a bastard!

No, no, you're being much too hard on the man. Perhaps he saw hypnotism as a harmless and practical solution to my sudden loss of confidence. This was live television, we were flying by the seats of our pants in the middle of an important production. There would have been no time to talk me through the problem as you might with a young actor today.

But Robin, it was a completely contemptible and immoral course of action that might have caused untold damage to you.

Not at all! The fact that I snapped out of it so quickly after the serial's completion probably indicates that I had been put under the 'fluence by a more than competent, indeed, extremely professional hypnotist. As a result of his efforts I did, after all, give a very good performance as Michael Summerwood.

'The Fountains of Time' was well liked by critics, viewers and by professionals in the business. It was a marvellous start to my career and opened all sorts of doors for me. Before the serial I was just another earnest child actor making a few pounds doing bits and pieces on the radio and newspaper and magazine adverts. After the serial was shown I immediately acquired an agent and job offers increased in quality and quantity. I have been in the business now for over fifty years and since 1954 I've hardly ever been out of work. I have Adrian Mackinder to thank for writing the enchanting book we serialised, and I have Lawrence England to thank for allowing me to surmount a crisis in mid-production and show what I was truly capable of. Now tell me, Jennifer what possible harm could there be in that?

FIVE

So between the completion of the 1954 'Fountains of Time' when you were a stripling actor of twelve and the beginning of the 1967 version by which time you had matured into a dashing leading man -

Correction! I became a leading man after the transmission of 'The Fountains of Time' in 1967. Before that you would have to describe me as an effective and in demand second-lead actor. I left school at fifteen and with my track record, a good agent and various bogus diplomas, personally awarded to me by Miss Molly Clackett, it was relatively easy to persuade my parents to allow me to enter the business full time.

Were they not 100% supportive anyway after your triumph on television?

Not really. They rather saw my acting as a sort of well-paid hobby, something I'd grow out of. My father still hankered after getting me a job in the City. He was very concerned at the uncertainty of regular employment that he rightly supposed was endemic in the acting profession.

But you've said that in fifty years, Robin, you were never out of work!
No, but then I was one of the lucky ones.

You had a fabulous career because you were very good at your job.
Nice of you to say that, Jennifer. I certainly had a positive talent and, much more importantly, an intelligence for acting in the first place; but in the end it all comes down to hard work, although I never saw what I did as work, not the sort of work my Dad did, it was always fun for me. I worked hard at drama school because I enjoyed it. When I left to enter the business full-time I prepared every part I took whether it was a thirty second voice-over or the lead in an Ibsen play down to the last detail. I never went into a rehearsal room without knowing my lines because I loved what I did and I wanted to do it as well as I could. I got work because producers and directors knew how punctilious and reliable I was. I must have stolen many a part from an actor more suited to a role simply because the people in charge knew they wouldn't have any trouble with me. I was never temperamental because I didn't forget my fortunate beginnings and I always felt grateful for being an actor and grateful to anyone who'd me pay me money to speak lines. It's true my last years were perhaps a little clouded shall we say with disenchantment but that's what happens when you

get on a bit. I retired at the right time, not like those old buggers who go on forever deluded into believing they still have 'something to offer' the public.

Right. It is a very long resumé with hundreds of stage, TV and film roles. What do you consider were the highlights of your early career up to the 1967 'Fountains of Time'?
As I told you when I left school I went into repertory theatre for two or three years and there learnt my craft. They were great times for a young actor and I picked up a tremendous amount but the standard of the productions was very variable. The company would be playing 'Three Sisters' in Bristol in the evenings for one week and rehearsing 'Charlie's Aunt' in the mornings for Huddersfield the following week. With the popularity of the cinema and the introduction of commercial television, rep was dying on its feet in the 1950s and it became quite impossible to maintain any kind of standard. I can tell you I was very relieved to get off that particular treadmill.

How did you manage to do this?
I had a very good agent called Phyllis Barnes who having insisted I go into rep in the first place whipped me out as soon as she reckoned I'd learned enough. By then I was getting lots of radio roles, some tellies and a fair few film parts and it was becoming harder to fit long tours in anyway.

And the money was better?
Of course! I returned to Lime Grove and did
a couple of series of 'Billy Bunter of Greyfriars
School' for BBC Television as one of Bunter's pals
in the Remove – you won't have heard of him –

**Yes I have! Billy Bunter was a greedy, stupid fat
kid, originally in 'The Magnet' – the children's
weekly that Adrian Mackinder unsuccessfully
wrote for.**
I'm impressed! Then there was a fairly long period
when I got rather typed as an unruly adolescent or
teenage thug in things like 'Dixon of Dock Green'
and 'Murder Squad' on television and there were
a few dreadful British 'B' pictures with titles like,
'Flick-knife Boy' and 'Cosh Boy' in which I would
firmly convince old ladies and nervous vicars into
believing that the fabric of society had entirely
disintegrated.

We called those 'problem movies' in the States.
The only problem with these films was that they
were crap. But the South London accent came in
handy and it was but a short step to affect a Northern or Midlands accent for more decent 'slice of
life' pictures when New-wave directors like Tony
Richardson, John Schlesinger and Karl Reisz came
along.

**You were in 'A Kind of Loving' and 'Saturday
Night and Sunday Morning'– great movies!**
Yes indeed, but I had quite small roles: Albert

Finney's drinking pal, and Alan Bates' younger brother. They both grew out of the Angry Young Men that had elbowed aside the plays of Coward and Rattigan from the London stage of course. I actually played Jimmy Porter at Bromley in 1961 – marvellous part, went like a bomb if I say so myself.

So there you were at the beginning of the Swinging Sixties: twenty-two years old with your dark saturnine good looks regularly beginning to appear on playbills and movie posters. What happened next?

What happened next was I got married.

To Christine Whelen, a young actress from Manchester.

We'd both been booked for a three month British Council tour of the Far East: five plays by Shakespeare, Sheridan, Wilde, Shaw and some awful modern piece that I've completely forgotten. We performed in town halls, converted cinemas, canvas marquees and jungle clearings. As you can imagine the fun soon palled what with the heat, flies, venomous snakes and every conceivable theatrical disaster possible. Christine and I were rather thrown together. That's not to say we didn't have real feelings for each other. After the Billie Gibson fiasco it took me a long time to regain my confidence where women were concerned and although there were a few casual girl friends during my rep period it was all a bit hit and miss. Chris-

tine and I were very alike in many ways: same
working class background, aspirations to better
ourselves, similar career path; we had something
very special between us and to this day I'm sorry
she divorced me in 1968.

Because of Hédi Gela?
Because of Hédi Gela. But we're running ahead
of ourselves. I sent my parents a telegram from
Singapore to tell them I'd married Christine. They
weren't best pleased as you can imagine: upset at
missing the wedding of their only son, but molli-
fied somewhat when our daughter, Katy was born
seven months later. Actually they both got on extremely well with Christine. My father adored her
and I got the most tremendous bollocking from
him when the ordure hit the fan in '67.

Where did you decide to live?
We found a very nice flat in Hammersmith overlooking the river. It was expensive but ideally
centred for work. My abiding impression of the
place was a huge radiogram-cum-cocktail cabinet
we had at one end of the lounge. People don't have
cocktail cabinets today, do they? – or radiograms
— and at least three silver cigarette boxes for our
friends, who all smoked like crematorium chim-
neys, to dip into. They're another thing that's
gone.

**Did Christine continue to work after she had
Katy?**

No, I think the British Council tour killed all enthusiasm for acting as far as she was concerned. She'd do the odd telly or film part if I could wangle one for her but she'd go for months without anything turning up and never minded. She'd glance through a copy of 'The Stage' and be delighted to read about her friends landing parts and doing well but when the kids came along she quite happily retired from the business.

Did you mind this?
Not at all, I was earning plenty of money for both of us and she was a marvellous mother to the kids.

How did she feel about you going on tours, location filming, that sort of thing?
She never minded, she trusted me, and I can tell you she had every reason to do so. I suppose it's harping back to the bloody Billie Gibson incident again, but after seeing BG standing with her knickers round her ankles, shaking like a jelly over Lawrence England's dead body I was always somewhat cynical and wary about consorting with the ladies of my profession. For me actresses broadly fall into two types: the ambitious ones and the lazy ones. Ambitious actresses will stun you with their looks and personality and demand that you fall in love with them, but in the end all they're interested in is achieving their professional aims. They make terrible lovers because they are invariably selfish and egotistical. The lazy ones see the business only as a stepping stone to something

else: social acclaim, a recording contract, marriage, opening a boutique or an antique shop, anything as long as they don't actually have to do any acting.

And what type was Christine?
Oh, the second. All she wanted to do was get married and have kids. She was delighted to give up acting. Nothing wrong with that of course. As I have said she was a very good wife to me and a wonderful mother to Katy and James.

So now on to the 1967 BBC serialisation of 'The Fountains of Time', six pre-recorded black and white episodes beginning on Sunday the 19th November with the final episode being shown on Christmas Eve.

5.15
   THE FOUNTAINS OF TIME
   An adventure serial in six episodes
   with
   DAVID TUDOR
   as Michael Summerwood
   and
   PENELOPE AVERELL
   as Susan Summerwood

   EPISODE ONE:

A STORY OF LOST TREASURE
by KEN ANDREWS
based on the novel by Adrian Mackinder

Cast:
Mr Summerwood...............Raymond Homfrey
Mrs Summerwood.........................June Rogers
Stationmaster...........................Sidney Baxter
Old Daniel...........................Warrington Lovat
Uncle Philip...........................Gregory Watson
Aunt Julie..Elaine Barton
First Fountain Spirit.....................Robin Glass
Second Fountain Spirit.....................Hédi Gela
Incidental music by Norman Deane
Story editor, Ramsey Brayton
Designer, Barry Gifford
Associate producer, Paul Potter
Producer, Jessie Fraser
Directed by Max Cooper

You miss out on top billing for the first episode because you're only on for a few seconds at the end.
Whether the idea to remake the serial came about because of Mackinder's death the previous year, I don't know, but I'm quite certain that the brainwave of bringing back the child actors from the 1954 production to play the Fountain Spirits and the other main roles was decided on at a very early

stage of production. It was considered to be not only a good publicity wheeze but it also chimed in nicely with the theme of character renewal in the novel. Not that anyone noticed this.

But as it turned out Anna Lombard was unavailable to return as the female Fountain Spirit.
Not in the first instance. She was in some dreadful farce in the West End that had been running for months and initially she didn't want to leave the production. The BBC offered to accommodate Anna by rescheduling rehearsals and recording to make things as easy as possible for her; and then madam's agent stuck out for some ridiculous money. The Beeb refused to agree since it would mean jacking up my money as well, but I did hear that future offers of work of an enticing nature were dangled before her management and finally La Lombard agreed to come aboard.

So what happened?
We filmed some inserts for the early episodes and rehearsed in a room at the Mary Wood Settlement for three weeks at the end of which Anna suddenly walked off the production.

Because?
The Press release said that her health had broken down due to pressure of work but she was back in her West End play a week later.

So what do you think the problem was?
I don't really know. She seemed all right in re-

hearsals – knew her lines, was reasonably co-operative with the cast and director. As I have indicated, she was a very temperamental type so perhaps the pressure of actually having to do some work for a change did get to her.

She wasn't upset by anything else?
What else could there be? We were all terribly sweet to her and I made a point of being particularly nice.

And so Hédi Gela was very much a last minute replacement?
Absolutely, but a very good one.

Were you pleased to be asked to play in 'The Fountains of Time' again?
Delighted. 1967 had been a very good year for me. I'd filmed an 'Avengers' episode for ABC in the spring where I'd played a very unpleasant villain and got to grapple with Diana Rigg in a haystack.

That was nice for you!
Yes, it wasn't bad. Then in the summer Tony Richardson very kindly remembered me for the part of a swinish British Officer in 'The Charge of the Light Brigade' with Vanessa Redgrave, his wife at the time, and the marvellous David Hemmings, which was entirely delightful. Then when I returned from location in Spain, Phyllis telephoned me to say the BBC wanted me for the lead in 'The Fountains of Time'.

Did you consider it to be your first major starring role?

I certainly did. You must understand that by 1967 BBC Children's television serials were winning huge audience figures. In 1954 when we'd gone out live with the first version hardly anyone had a television set in this country, but by 1967 every home had one and a quality drama production at five o'clock on a Sunday evening was considered to be prime viewing time. For that first episode in November we drew about eight million viewers. By the time the last episode was aired on Christmas Eve we had something approaching twenty million people looking in.

But there would have been an additional interest caused by the death of Hédi Gela before the showing of that last episode.

Yes, yes, of course, but what I'm trying to get across is how big a success the show was and, since you were kind enough to enquire, how it helped to move my acting career to another level.

I'm sorry, Robin, I didn't mean to say that 'The Fountains of Time' was only popular because Hédi was killed during the making of it.

I know that, Jennifer, and I didn't mean to crow that we got massive audience figures just because I was in it. Hédi was absolutely bloody brilliant in the serial and no one can ever take that away from her. It was a criminal tragedy that some managerial idiot at the BBC had the tapes wiped in the 1970s. I hate to imagine what God-awful-show they recorded over them.

There are lots of still photographs.
Yes, and there's a two-minute segment remaining from episode four which was used in a BBC training film, but honestly they give no idea how incredibly good Hédi was in all the episodes.

When did you first meet Hédi?
Not until the actual taping of the first episode on the 6th November. As soon as Hédi agreed to do the serial she was whisked away to retake all the film inserts that the director had shot with Anna Lombard. In episode one we were only needed for the final thirty seconds when the Fountain Spirits come alive which didn't need vast amounts of rehearsal. In the 1954 version it was too complicated to make the stone figures animate as in the book, but in 1967 with four years of 'Dr Who' technology it was a piece of cake.

Who is Dr Who?
I'm sorry, I thought he'd appeared in the States long ago: 'Dr Who' was a Sixties BBC science fiction series – also about time travel — that used groundbreaking special effects. Anyway Hédi and I met on the set at the Television Centre at White City on that Monday afternoon.

What were your first impressions of her?
Tall, lovely looking girl, black hair, nice figure,

very nice face, intelligent eyes which glistened, vivacious without overdoing it, friendly, very nicely spoken, perfect English – when they told me they'd engaged a Hungarian actress I thought she'd have an accent as thick as Zsa Zsa Gabor's.

She'd escaped from Hungry with her father in 1956 when she was fourteen years old and went to St. Paul's School, for Girls.

Yes, St. Paul's was just down the road from where Christine and I had our flat in Hammersmith. We often used to see the gels with their immaculately smart satchels and brief cases: very refeened young ladies. She knew only a little English before she came to this country and I imagine Hédi must have had quite a lot of extra tuition to make her talk like the other girls.

Did she affect a cut-glass English accent?

Not at all, I didn't mean to say she spoke affect-edly. No, she was entirely natural in her speech and manner. She had rather a contralto voice – slightly deep but without being boomy.

Sexy?

Hmmm, not a blatant come-on like Billie Gibson, but yes, I thought her voice was sexy – but then I thought everything about her was sexy.

OK, Robin, so you admit you were attracted to Hédi, which is apparent from the interviews I made recently with surviving cast and crew-members on the production and is completely

**obvious from the photographs I have of the two
of you together. Are you still going to deny there
was nothing between you?**

I'm not going to deny anything! Of course there
was something between us but it wasn't how you
and the rest of the world might like to think it
was. I never had an affair with Hédi — I very much
regret to say — but believe me it wasn't for the
want of trying.

Did you know that like you Hédi also kept a diary?
She told me about it but never showed me anything she'd written. I never showed her any of my
writing either come to that. Her diary was lost
wasn't it? I've never seen anything published from
it.

I have it with me here.
Good Lord!

**It was sent back after Hédi's death to her mother
in Hungry with her other effects. Her mother
couldn't understand English so I was the first
person to read Hédi's diary since 1967. I'm hoping her frank and unpublished comments about
her life as a young actress in England will give my
biography a head start over any rivals that may
swarm into the field when news breaks about my
book.**

I'm sure you are. Blimey, what does she say about
me?

I'll show you mine if you show me yours!

I think you're setting me up for something Jennifer, and I'm not sure I want to go where you want to take me.

Oh, come on, Robin, I'm not out to ambush you, honestly! Let's compare entries for the first day you and Hédi met. If you're not happy about sharing confidences we can simply drop it.
Very well, but under protest. Heavens, it's nearly forty years ago but I hope all this isn't going to reduce me to a blubbering wreck.

You'll be just fine, Robin!
Ok, it'll stiffen my resolve if I go first:

6/11/67

To Television Centre for taping first episode of 'The Fountains of Time' – stone costume very unwieldy with little room to breathe and a very uncomfortable makeup. Fortunately today is the first and also the last time I shall need to wear it. The cast is gelling nicely: Raymond Homfrey who I worked with in 'The Great Escape' movie and who is an extremely pleasant bloke is a natural, and Elaine Barton who was so marvellous in that terrible Tennessee Williams play we did at Chichester two seasons ago is again excellent. I'm glad Max Cooper is directing, he's efficient, takes no bloody nonsense from anyone but has a wonderful eye for those little details that make the difference between an adequate production and an exciting one. Talking of excitement, my new co-star, the Hungarian-born, Hédi Gela is something of a find! How odd it is when casting suddenly comes up with someone who exactly fits the image of a character one had formed from reading the book. Unlike Anna Lombard, who was perfectly all right but perhaps a little too straight in the part, this one seems to have something extra about her and I'm sure she will do well in her role. Begin rehearsing in earnest tomorrow!

Now my turn:

Monday, November 6th 1967

The new curtains arrived this morning and I spent a happy couple of hours putting them up and making the finishing touches to the flat. I'm very pleased with the way things look and think I shall be very content here. Another letter from Mother! She is still upset about Father's death and does not like the idea of me living in London by myself! I will write to her tomorrow. I took a taxi to the Television Centre in the afternoon to do the first tiny bit of filming – sorry taping! – of the children's serial, 'The Fountains of Time'. The cast seem nice, apart from Warrington Lovat who is an old goat. Robin Glass, my co-star is very handsome but rather intense. Someone told me he is married! I'm looking forward to beginning work properly tomorrow. Studied lines then to the Festival Hall in the evening with Ruth: Beethoven's Ninth conducted by Klemperer – the slow movement was too slow but the finale was sublime!

Now that didn't hurt a bit did it, Robin?
I remember those bloody curtains! It was a nice flat, and before you ask, yes I did visit it. She was right about Warrington Lovat who played Old Daniel: a Lawrence England clone – but not as nice — who, like him, couldn't keep his flies done up. What is it about elderly male actors always being depraved paedophiles or randy old stoats? Must have been something to do with playing the part of Old Daniel.

Hédi called him an old goat not an old stoat!
Same difference. It's nice to hear how Hédi was looking forward to working at the Beeb. You know she'd never done television before? Straight into movies from RADA! I think there were one or two stage roles in her tragically brief career but the camera loved her face and she would surely have gone on to become a major film and television actress.

The half a dozen movies she completed have become minor classics in my opinion because of her presence in them.
Yes, even that dreadful comedy she did with Charlie Drake – amazing what dying young will do for the posthumous reputation.

Passing quickly over that remark, tell me about the Tuesday when you had your first full day of

rehearsal together.
It was a complicated set-up where the Fountain
Ghosts take the two children on a wild horseback ride at night across Dartmoor. Although
special effects technology had advanced considerably since 1954, we still had dummy horses to sit
on and what today would be considered a rather
primitive means of back-projection. It's an essen-
tial and exciting scene but actually I've always
thought it came across more effectively in the
novel.

There came a massive flash of lightening and
in an instant two huge white horses suddenly appeared in the rose garden, their front legs rearing
up, their hind legs tramping backwards into the
rose beds, tails flailing rose leaves into the air, the
animals' great black eyes rolling as if completely
demented. Susan shrank further into Michael's
arms, terrified, and even he felt his natural courage begin to wane at such an alarming apparition.
The He-spirit seeing the children's fear laughed rather unkindly then helped his ghostly companion
onto her charger. The She-spirit, Susan noticed,
while very beautiful had an almost sullen and ab-
stracted look on her face as if she would prefer to
be elsewhere rather than helping two frightened
children to look for some tiresome treasure that
held no interest for her. But what, Susan won-

dered, would the lovely ghost rather have been doing?

"Are you two coming or not?" bellowed the He-spirit above the sound of rain and thunder and he leapt onto the saddle of his steed and brought the animal alongside the fountain. Michael rose reluctantly from the wall and in one swift movement the ghost swept the boy onto the horse's neck and pulled him roughly into his arms. Susan, suddenly afraid at being left behind ran towards the She-spirit's horse and she too was picked up as if she had been as light as one of the garden's fluttering rose petals. She looked down at the hand that held her waist so tightly and noticed that each phantom finger was beringed with a different coloured stone which flashed in the lightening and that the ghost's finger nails were long, pointed and pale like the talons of some enormous hunting bird.

There was another huge clap of thunder and as Michael's horse reared up the He-spirit snapped his rein and shouted some unintelligible command into the beast's raised and twitching ears. Michael wondered how the enormous horse and rider would pass under the rose garden's walled doorway that was only high enough for a man of average height like Uncle Philip to walk through. The horses began to canter not towards the door but in the opposite direction, clattering along the paving-stoned path towards the eight-foot high redbrick wall at the other end of the garden. The horses suddenly picked up speed and he heard the beginnings of a scream from his sister behind him and his own mouth fell open but he could make no sound. As the wall raced up towards them the He-spirit pulled hard on his rein and Michael felt the horse give a tremendously powerful kick with its hind legs. The animal seemed to rise almost vertically from the ground and to his astonishment Michael looked down as the wall fell away beneath them. Even more astonishing, once over the obstacle, horse and riders did not drop to the ground but carried on careering through the air some twelve or fifteen feet above Uncle Philip's croquet lawn on the other side of the rose garden.

The He-spirit laughed again as he made his charger gallop alongside the ivy-clad walls of Monckton Manor where he pulled up outside Michael's bedroom on the first floor so that the boy could stare in through the window and see the night-light still burning beside his empty bed.

"Want to go back, Michael?" the spirit breathed icily into Michael's ear. "Back to bed and back to sleep to wake in the morning with all this but a fantastic, half-remembered dream?"

Michael looked over to his sister, whose great horse was pawing the empty air with its front legs as if it couldn't wait to begin the midnight ride. A white-faced Susan, clutched in the arms of the impassive She-spirit looked back anxiously towards her brother but with the fear he also saw in her eyes a positive glint of excitement.

"No," said Michael firmly looking up into the mask-like face of the spirit whose eyes gleamed with mischief, "you promised to take us to where the Monks' treasure was hidden. You have been sent to us by an enchantment to do that very thing and I do not think you can break your promise."

"Ha! Neither can I, boy! You speak bravely but ignorantly, you do not understand for what you ask. Very well, if that is what you truly wish then I must take you to that place where I and my sister concealed the Holy gold from Henry VIII's thievish soldiers and where we paid for such diligence with our lives."

"You were the son and daughter of a great Catholic nobleman as in the story we were told?" asked Michael, his eyes suddenly alive with admiration.

"Or the thieving couple who gulled the Holy monks into handing over their treasures so that we might live the lives of the nobility you believe us to be!" roared the spirit, and he cracked the reins sharply making his great white charger rear up before it tore off into the black night.

For the next two hours the two great horses galloped abreast of each other, their hooves sweeping the air a house's height above the darkened countryside. The rain had ceased but thunder still rumbled away in the distance and the odd flash of lightening illuminated empty summer fields and deserted roads and pathways below them. Michael found it quite impossible to get used to the fact that his horse was travelling through the air instead of cantering across solid ground. It was extremely peculiar because whenever they approached a clump of tall trees Michael could never predict how his steed would react. Sometimes the beast would gain height and simply fly over the treetops; at other times the animal seemed to prefer to circumnavigate the obstruction. Once, when they approached what seemed to be a copse of tall fir trees, the horse charged through the tree trunks, branches and foliage as if they hadn't been there. It wasn't logical thought Michael, but why should it be? And why was there a constant noisy drumming of horses' hooves in his ear when the animal wasn't actually moving along the ground?

After one particularly spectacular acrobatic manoeuvre by the phantom charger, Michael had nearly tumbled from the horse's neck and had frozen in terror as the ghost's hand had unceremoniously hauled him back upright.

"What are you frightened of, boy?" the spirit laughed, "do you think you could fall and be killed?"

"The horse is travelling very quickly and we are so far from the ground, anyone might be afraid."

"Afraid, Michael? What is there to be afraid of when neither I, nor the horse can possibly exist? Unlike your sister I thought you were the rational thinker who didn't believe in ghosts or any kind of supernatural happenings, isn't that so?"

Michael nodded stupidly but he still hung on to the horse's mane for dear life. What difference did it make if ghosts existed or not when you were thundering along twenty feet above the ground at thirty-five miles an hour?

Susan had seen her brother talking to the He-spirit and felt very uncomfortable that so far the ghostly figure whose arm clasped her waist had spoken not a single word to her. She sat for a long time trying to think of something intelligent to open a possible conversation – a 'conversational ice-breaker' her mother would have called it – but absolutely nothing remotely suitable entered her head. What do you say to a beautiful female spirit as you sit together on a great white horse flying through the air? What a stormy night! But don't you think we are having a splendid summer? I see you have a lovely horse, what do you call it? How far are we going? Will we soon be there? What a perfectly lovely white dress you are wearing, did you make it yourself or buy it in a shop?

Perhaps if she turned round to look at the ghost the spirit might speak to her first. Susan bit her lip in frustration: if finding something sensible to say to the lady had proved to be too difficult, physically turning her head round suddenly seemed a complete impossibility. She tried very hard but found she did not have the will to perform the simple action of turning her face and looking upwards. What was this strange and powerful force that kept her head facing into the onrushing night air? When she found she couldn't move her head that became the one thing in all the world she wanted to do.

Susan realised angrily that the ghost was probably doing it on purpose: making her sit still so that she wouldn't fall off the horse or, more likely, because the phantom horsewoman couldn't be bothered to chatter to some stupid little girl. But Susan had always been very determined and stubborn; if the ghost was exercising some sort of willpower over her then she must use her own strength of mind and personality to overturn the spell. She took a deep breath, closed her eyes and concentrated very hard on saying a simple mantra to herself: I must turn my head round and look at her face! I must turn my head round and look at her face! I must turn my head round and look at her face!

Over and over again she repeated the words and as she did so she felt a strange energy begin to stir deep inside her. It started somewhere in her stomach and began to rise through her arms and chest until it reached her shoulders and then started to seep into the muscles of her neck. I must turn my head round and look at her face! I must turn my head round and look at her face! I must turn my head round! Suddenly she knew she would be able to do it. Susan opened her eyes, took a deep breath . . . and looked round into the face of the ghost!

The phantom's head seemed impossibly large to her, like the wooden figure on the prow of a sailing ship or a medieval carving of the Madonna on a cathedral wall. The deep brown eyes were certainly very big: they glistened and stared forward towards the horizon. The young woman had extremely pale skin but it was not so white or transparent, Susan decided, that it did not look human. Although she knew she was looking up at the face of a ghost, she did not feel as though the face was corpse-like or in any way long dead. It was inanimate but Susan felt this was through choice rather than a natural state of things. The lady's short curly black hair was luxuriant and bristled in the wind – it was very beautiful, Susan thought, and the richness of its sheen belied its ghostliness. Didn't ghosts all have straggly white or grey hair?

There was no trace of makeup on the face which, thought Susan, was hardly surprising, but still the lips had a natural fullness and redness that reminded her of some of the fashion photographs she'd seen in her mother's magazines. There was a similar haughtiness, an unspoken acknowledge-

ment of personal beauty, a sense of feminine un-
attainability that Susan also associated with one
or two continental film actresses that her father
confessed to admiring.

Quite suddenly those large brown eyes
swivelled down to look at Susan and fixedly held
her gaze. What was there to read in them? Susan
believed that she could always tell what people
were thinking and was often reprimanded by
adults for her habit of staring enquiringly into
people's faces. But here there was absolutely nothing to read. The eyes seemed huge but as empty
of life, feelings and anything resembling human
emotion as could be. Susan turned her face back
into the wind and found her own thoughts and
feelings had become as blank as that beautiful face
had been.

At last, as the first rays of the sun began to
redden the horizon, the horses slowed their furious pace, and looking down the children could
see a clearing among the trees where there was a
slowly flowing stream and an old stone bridge.

5. EXT.STONE BRIDGE. STUDIO. DAY

(THE HE-SPIRIT TIES HIS HORSE TO A TREE
THEN HELPS MICHAEL TO DISMOUNT. WE PULL
BACK TO DISCOVER THE SHE-SPIRIT SITTING
ON A TREE STUMP DISTRACTEDLY EXAMINING
HER FINGER NAILS AS SUSAN LIES NEARBY ON

THE RIVER BANK SPLASHING HER HAND IN THE WATER.)

SHE-SPIRIT: If you splash my dress I shall be extremely cross.

SUSAN: I think I can see a treasure chest lying on the riverbed!

SHE-SPIRIT: Idiot!

MICHAEL: (RUNNING QUICKLY TO LOOK INTO THE STREAM) Where? Let me see, Susan!

HE-SPIRIT: You're wasting your time; we didn't hide the treasure in the river, it would be far too easy to find.

MICHAEL: (EXCITEDLY) The bridge! It's somewhere under the bridge!

(HE SPLASHES IMPULSIVELY INTO THE SHALLOW STREAM AND BEGINS TO SEARCH BENEATH THE BRIDGE'S ARCH)

There's a loose stone here – I'm sure I can lift it out!

SUSAN: Do be careful, Michael!

SHE-SPIRIT: Just look at the foolish boy!

HE-SPIRIT: (LAUGHING) Full marks for finding my secret niche but you don't honestly think the treasure's still hidden there do you?

MICHAEL: (EMERGING WET AND ANGRY FROM

BENEATH THE BRIDGE) But you said you would show us where the treasure was hidden. You promised!

HE-SPIRIT: I promised to show you where we hid the treasure. I didn't promise it would still be there four hundred years later!

SUSAN: What a dreadful swizzle!

MICHAEL: I think that's a rotten trick!

SHE-SPIRIT: (RISING ANGRILY AND STABBING MICHAEL ROUGHLY WITH HER FINGER) How dare you say such a thing! My brother and I were hounded like wolves for that treasure. Why, I was attacked by thirty ruffians with swords and nearly had my head cut off!

HE-SPIRIT: (PUTTING HIS ARM AROUND HER) So you did, my dear, and you were very brave. Unfortunately these two silly ingrates have no idea what we went through. (TO THE CHILDREN) We'd been riding all night, hotly pursued by Henry's soldiers and then my sister's horse became lame and we had to transfer the treasure to my horse and walk the rest of the way.

6. EXT.STONE BRIDGE. STUDIO. DAY
(WITH A DISSOLVE EDIT THE TWO GHOSTS, NOW AS THEIR FORMER SELVES, SIR ROGER DE FREECE AND LADY ANNE DE FREECE WEARILY LEAD THEIR TREASURE-LADEN HORSE ACROSS THE BRIDGE)

LADY ANNE: It's no good, Roger, I cannot walk a step further.

SIR ROGER: It is but a mile to the house, if we can make that refuge our friends and servants will protect us from the mob. (SHE COLLAPSES INTO HIS ARMS) But I see I have already asked too much of you. Dear Anne, sit down here on the bridge and rest. I think I have an idea. (HE JUMPS INTO THE STREAM AND BEGINS TO EXAMINE THE UNDERSIDE OF THE BRIDGE) Above the stream, I remember, there is a loose stone with a cavity behind it. We will dispose of the gold beneath this arch and return when the soldiers have given up their search. Pass me down the saddlebags, Anne – it will take but a moment.

(LADY ANNE UNSTRAPS THE SADDLEBAGS AND LOWERS THEM OVER THE SIDE OF THE BRIDGE FOR SIR ROGER TO CONCEAL THE TREASURE. HE DOES SO NOT A MOMENT TOO SOON BECAUSE THERE IS HEARD THE SOUND OF APPROACHING RIDERS)

LADY ANNE: Quickly Roger, they are almost upon us!

(SIR ROGER LIFTS LADY ANNE ONTO THE HORSE AND QUICKLY MOUNTING UP HIMSELF THE FUGATIVES DISAPPEAR THROUGH THE TREES AND WE PULL BACK AGAIN TO SEE THEM ONCE MORE AS GHOSTS.

7. EXT.STONE BRIDGE. STUDIO. DAY

(THEY ARE NOW BOTH SEATED ON THE TREE STUMP, THE HE-SPIRIT WITH HIS ARM AROUND HIS SISTER WHO IS DABBING HER EYES WITH A HANDKERCHIEF)

SHE-SPIRIT: I was twenty-three years old and engaged to be married to the most eligible nobleman in Devon and Cornwall – then this had to happen!

HE-SPIRIT: The soldiers caught up with up with us before we could reach safety and we were no match for their numbers.

SHE-SPIRIT: But you fought so bravely darling!

HE SPIRIT: I was unable to defend my sister or myself and the mob cut us down as if we had been vermin.

SHE-SPIRIT: (NOW PUTTING A CONSOLING ARM AROUND HIM) Oh, but you did your best, Roger, and I was proud of the way you carried yourself in the most taxing of circumstances.

SUSAN: But what happened to the treasure?

HE-SPIRIT: (ICILY) I beg your pardon?

MICHAEL: (GUILTILY) My sister . . . we were both wondering what happened to the treasure.

SHE SPIRIT: (FURIOUS) My brother and I have our

heads cut off – well, almost cut off – and all you can say is 'what happened to the treasure?'

HE-SPIRIT: Yes, I have to agree with my sister, I do think your remarks are rather impolite and certainly tasteless but I suppose that is what we must expect from the youth of today.

MICHAEL: I'm sorry.

SUSAN: (QUICKLY) I'm sorry too but your story was so exciting I couldn't wait to find out what happened in the end.

HE-SPIRIT: I see, well since you put it like that it is quite a tale.

SHE-SPIRIT: That terrible vulgar man!

HE-SPIRIT: And that perfectly awful woman who went as his wife!

8. EXT. STONE BRIDGE. STUDIO. DAY

(ANOTHER DISSOLVE EDIT SEES THE TWO PHANTOMS GOT UP AS CAPTAIN BLOOD AND HIS BLOUSY PARAMOUR, MADELEINE, CROSSING THE BRIDGE ON TWO DONKEYS. THEY ARE IN EXTREMELY HIGH SPIRITS – POSSIBLY INTOXICATED BY ALCOHOL – LOUDLY SINGING, JOKING AND LAUGHING. HE IS WEARING A VERY LARGE AND SILLY HAT WHICH MADELEINE IS ATTEMPTING TO KNOCK INTO THE STREAM)

BLOOD: Hold hard, madam, you will have my crowning glory in the water!

MADELEINE: Which is the best place for it! I declare no man ever wore a sillier thing on his head!

BLOOD: But it is in the highest of fashions!

MADELEINE: (ATTEMPTING ANOTHER LUNGE AT THE HAT) It is certainly very high and I think it should be brought very low!

(THE HAT IS KNOCKED INTO THE WATER AND FLOATS UNDER THE BRIDGE)

BLOOD: (HURRIDLY DISMOUNTING AND LOOKING FIRST ON ONE SIDE OF THE BRIDGE THEN THE OTHER) But I cannot see it!

MADELEINE: (LAUGHING HYSTERICALLY) It's stuck! Your beautiful hat is so large it had become wedged under the bridge!

BLOOD: And now I suppose I must get my stockings wet to retrieve it!

MADELEINE: Oh, leave it for the fishes, I promise to buy you another.

BLOOD: (PULLING OFF SHOES AND STOCKINGS) You'll never buy another hat like that one!

MADELEINE: That most certainly is true: the fool who made it was almost a greater fool than the fool who paid good money for it!

(BLOOD WADES INTO THE STREAM AND DISAP-
PEARS FOR A LONG TIME BENEATH THE BRIDGE)

MADELEINE: (CONCERNED) Thomas! Are you
there my angel? Tommy? It is very cruel of you to
hide from your Madeleine like this. I didn't mean
what I said about your hat – it is a beautiful hat – it
is the finest, most distinguished – Oh, Thomas!

(A DUMBFOUNDED BLOOD EMERGES FROM THE
ARCH OF THE BRIDGE CARRYING HIS HAT WHICH
IS LADEN WITH TREASURE)

9. EXT.STONE BRIDGE. STUDIO. DAY

MICHAEL: Was this the same Captain Blood who
later broke into the Tower of London and tried to
steal Charles II's Crown Jewels?

HE-SPIRIT: The very same man. And to practice
stealing from the King, the scoundrel first stole
my treasure!

SHE-SPIRIT: Our treasure, darling.

SUSAN: Actually didn't it belong to the monks?

HE-SPIRIT: Well, all right, the monk's treasure,
but the fact is that appallingly vulgar man stole it.

MICHAEL: But can't we stop them?

10. EXT.STONE BRIDGE. STUDIO. DAY

(WHISTLING AND LAUGHING BLOOD AND MAD-

ELEINE ARE HAPPILY LOADING THE TREASURE ONTO ONE OF THE DONKEYS)

BLOOD: Now I shall buy a hundred hats!

MADELEINE: And what shall you buy me, my love?

BLOOD: A golden coach with eighteen horses, two lackeys to drive them and a maid to powder your darling face, my angel!

MADELEINE: Oh Tommy, I'm sure that I shall presently swoon!

BLOOD: Hold thy swooning until we get the loot beneath our bed, My beloved, I fear if we are observed some knave will try to steal our boon and turn our good fortune to nothing!

11. EXT.STONE BRIDGE. STUDIO. DAY

HE-SPIRIT: Of course we can't stop them! These things I show you are visions that happened hundreds of years ago.

SUSAN: Then the treasure is lost?

(THE FOUNTAIN SPIRITS LOOK MEANINGFULLY AT EACH OTHER)

MICHAEL: If you can show us what happened when you lost the treasure then surely you must be able to show us what Captain Blood did with it next?

SHE-SPIRIT: (CUPPING HER CHIN IN HER HANDS)
Oh dear, I was rather afraid he was going to say
that!

SIX

You and Hédi must have found it hard work playing all these varied characters in a tight shooting schedule. Was the suggestion ever made that some of these might be played by different actors?

In the live 1954 version it just wasn't possible for the actors playing the Fountain Spirits to play the other parts as well, but in the book it is implicit that most of the adult characters in the story are projections of the two ghosts and when we came to remake the novel in 1967 the techniques were there for us to do this. If you look at that scene by the stone bridge for instance, within the space of five minutes Hédi plays the moody She-spirit, the terrified Lady Anne de Freece and the strumpet, Madeleine — and she played them all marvellously. This was a very complicated set-up that took us the best part of a day to record. The fun of the piece, for the actors and the viewers, was seeing all these very different characters played by just two performers. Yes, it was a bit of a slog and I wouldn't like to take something on like that today, but then we were both young, energetic and at the peak of our careers.

It was certainly Hédi's last role but I'm surprised you should consider 'The Fountains of Time' to have been the peak of your career. What about all the other stuff – the Hammer Horrors and leading film and television roles you did afterwards?

No, it was mostly rubbish! I did some Shakespeare when I was in my fifties that I'm proud of because – all modesty aside — it was pretty damn good, but the best thing I did when I was young, handsome and in my pomp was 'The Fountains of Time'.

What was Hédi like to work with on set?

Very good, very professional, technically excellent. Always knew her lines and marks. She could take direction without any fuss but would make sensible suggestions if she felt they would improve the piece without putting people's backs up. She was a very natural actor – most people in this business aren't. She was a very good mimic and could do any number of accents, but I think her secret was observation. She was always looking at how people behaved and reacted, but nothing was just parroted back, she would put her own creative slant on characters, flesh them out fully, make them seem entirely real. She was an extremely hardworking girl, liked doing lots of research, liked working overtime, always pleased to do another take, always gave a 1000%. She was a good old trouper too, didn't put on any side even though she was quite rightly the star of the show. Had a lovely attitude and manner on the set – chatted away to extras and tea ladies which not all actors can be bothered to do.

I bet you did, Robin.
Yes, certainly. Hédi and I shared a similar work ethic and outlook on the profession and life in general which I suppose must have influenced the BBC's decision to cast us together.

You were soul mates.
I thought so. I wanted so much that we should get together, but there you go, you make mistakes in life – things happen, you have to live with them.

At least you got to see the new curtains in her flat. How did that come about?
Music! After we'd finally finished taping all those complicated bits in episode two and watched the recording a few days before transmission, she mentioned that she liked the opening and clos-ing music to the serial and where could she buy a record of it. I told her that it was the same music they'd used in 1954 – quite untrue – and that I had an LP that I'd be delighted to lend her. As a ploy to get her into bed it was pathetic but I've found that all such ploys are pathetic and all have an equal chance of success. Anyway I took the produ-cer's P.A. to one side and asked her what the piece was – it was by Elgar, the 'Fountain Dance' from his 'Wand of Youth Suite' – and dashed down to HMV's

in Oxford Street to buy a copy to loan to Hédi.

Sneaky!

My musical preferences in those days I'm afraid
were typically show-biz and not very intellectual: Broadway musicals, Peggy Lee, Frank Sin-
atra, classic jazz and swing, a bit of Brubeck, very
much the sort of thing you'd expect from a busy
jobbing actor. I'd liked and collected some of the
orchestral soundtracks of the films I'd been in but
basically the world of classical music was a closed
book to me. When I lent Hédi the music of the
English composer, Elgar, she returned the compliment with the 'Music for Strings, Percussion and
Celesta' by the Hungarian, Bela Bartok. Although
she had been living in this country for over ten
years and had become naturalised she still liked to
preserve her Hungarian roots.

And how did you get on with Mr Bartok?

Played the record once – couldn't make head nor
tail of it. Played it twice – the same. Put it on for a
third time as I was getting dressed to go to the theatre with Christine one evening and it hit me like
a rocket – fabulous piece. I asked Hédi to lend me
something else by Bartok and she invited me up
to her flat to look through her record collection.
She'd just bought the cream Citroen Traction-
Avant out of her BBC cheque – her 'Maigret Motor',
the same model was featured in a very popular
series over here about Simenon's detective — and
we hared to and from the Television Centre one

lunchtime to pick up the LP. And before you ask there wasn't time for any funny business.

Perish the thought. You were emotionally involved with Hédi by that time and you would have been receptive to the things she liked.
Naturally, but I had also reached a period in my life when I'd begun to look more deeply into the arts. With music for instance, the old Broadway belters I'd learned at Molly Clackett's Drama Academy had finally begun to pall. I was looking for something a bit different culturally. I'd started to read some decent literature: the Germans, Hesse and Thomas Mann; the French Symbolist poets; the new English boys: Hughes, Gunn and Philip Larkin. My tastes were broadening and getting deeper. Meeting Hédi was a revelation because she had all this fabulous cultural baggage that was to me uncharted territory and I was eager to lap it up.

You wanted to lap Hédi Gela up!
True!

How did you square being married to Christine and having two young children while all this record swapping was going on?
A thoroughly impudent but fair question in the circumstances and the answer is that if I was being sneaky in trying to seduce Hédi I was being sneaky to myself at the same time because I was hardly aware of what I was doing.

Oh, come on, Robin!

No really! I was hugely busy doing 'The Fountains of Time'. My waking thoughts were 98% on making a success of the production. I assure you I did not fantasise about going to bed with Hédi Gela. I didn't even think of it on a conscious level. I believed I was making a good friend of someone who I admired as an artist and who I liked very much as a person. Of course beneath all this my genes were saying something very different and my libido was doing cartwheels.

And what about your marriage to Christine?

As I've told you, it was a happy marriage. I honestly wasn't looking for anyone else, and as I told you in the years we were together I never once strayed. Of course there had been opportunities: various actresses – some of them stunning – had taken a fancy to me, but I found, and find, a tremendous amount of women in show-business to be a complete turn off. There were some nice ones who might have been receptive to my attentions but you know I was never a predatory male as far as sex was concerned – good acting roles, yes – I'm not a saint but it simply wasn't my style, probably suffer from a low libido or something. If I'm to be perfectly honest, Christine wasn't the love of all time but I was very happy living with my wife and my kids and wouldn't have risked endangering my marriage for a bit on the side.

When did you first realise that you were in love with Hédi?

On set I'm afraid, and in the middle of a clinch – very unprofessional! In episode three I played Beau Brummel and Hédi played my mistress, Lady Charlotte somebody-or-other. They've acquired the monks' treasure in a card game and are about to leave one July evening for a night of gaiety in the Vauxhall Gardens. There was just the one kiss on Brummel's Regency sofa and the electricity was very tangible.

But you must have kissed lots of nice looking actresses before.

Dozens of 'em, but they meant absolutely nothing to me. It was just work, and sometimes it was bleedin' hard work! The public see sex scenes for actors as an extremely attractive perk of the job but I never knew an actor who didn't get embarrassed doing them. I'd been worried about that bloody kiss all day – worried that my feelings might get the better of me. In rehearsals Hédi and I had just laughed and faked things together, lightly brushing cheeks, that sort of thing, which was bad enough for the old emotions. If you start snogging big-time in draughty rehearsal rooms people are inclined to talk. I thought by getting completely into costume and character I could distance myself from the inner turmoil, and with the powdered wig and over-the-top outfit on I certainly felt the part. But as soon as I took Hédi into my arms, old Brummel smartly buggered off leaving an extremely vulnerable Robin Glass to go through with the smacker.

Describe!

Hédi was wearing this gorgeous green satin dress circa 1800 that the costume department had copied faithfully from some contemporary print. The bosoms were raised provocatively with the waist cut in tightly ... and incidentally did I mention to you that Hédi was exactly the right height for me? I remember old Lawrence England once saying on the set of the 1954 'Fountains of Time', 'When you get married, Robin, always make sure your wife is the correct height for you. Don't go for a girl that's too tall or too short. You should be able to look down into her eyes and the tip of your nose should touch her the top of her forehead and her breasts should meet three-quarters up your ribcage'. Silly old bugger! God knows where he'd dug that idea up from! And what was he doing telling a twelve year-old boy all this? Anyway our lips met precisely on cue – held for the regulation BBC three seconds – then parted. It was the first time I would kiss Hédi, and also the last time. It was intensely pleasurable but with the kiss came the revelation that I was now in love with Hédi, which was entirely earth shattering.

9. INT. BEAU'S MAYFAIR HOME. STUDIO. NIGHT

(BRUMMEL AND HIS MISTRESS, LADY CHAR-
LOTTE ARE SEATED TOGETHER ON A CHAISE
LONGUE GAZING LOVINGLY INTO EACH
OTHER'S EYES.)

BEAU: Oh Lady Charlotte!

LADY CHARLOTTE: Oh Beau!

BEAU: My darling Charley!

LADY CHARLOTTE: My sweet Georgie-worgie-
porgie!

(THEY ARE ABOUT TO KISS BUT ARE INTER-
RUPTED BY BRUMMEL'S MANSERVANT, CAR-
STAIRS, WHO DISCREETLY CLEARS HIS THROAT)

BEAU: (SHARPLY) What ever is it, Carstairs?

CARSTAIRS: (ULTRA REFINED) A young gentleman and a young lady by the name of Michael
Summerwood and Susan Summerwood have
asked if they might see you for a few moments, sir.

BEAU: Summerwood, Summerwood? I don't
think I know the name. Wait a moment would
that be the Summerwoods of Worcestershire?

CARSTAIRS: I've no idea, sir.

BEAU: Well, I suppose you'd better show them in,
Carstairs. (TO LADY CHARLOTTE) I'm sorry about
this my angel, but it could be news about my Great
Aunt Sophia who lives in Hereford and is reputed

to be ailing.

LADY CHARLOTTE: (RISING AND SMOOTHING HER DRESS) Then of course you must see your visitors, Beau. They might be the bearers of good news about your unfortunate Great Aunt's demise and good news is the one thing we cannot have enough of.

(MICHAEL AND SUSAN STILL DRESSED IN PYJA-MAS ARE USHERED IN BY CARSTAIRS)

BEAU: Upon my word, they are children!

MICHAEL: Good evening, Mr Brummel.

SUSAN: Good evening Mr Brummel and Miss ...

LADY CHARLOTTE: (WALKING ROUND THEM AND STARING RUDELY) And most peculiar look-ing children too! I can hardly believe that such personages could be the bearers of any tidings worth the hearing.

BEAU: I'm afraid you might be right, my dear. Ask the wretches what they want.

MICHAEL: We've come to –

LADY CHARLOTTE: (SNAPPING HER FAN IN MICHAEL'S FACE) You heard what Mr Brummel said, now why have you come at this disgracefully late hour to disturb him?

BEAU: (RAISING ORNATE LORGNETTE AND STAR-

ING HARD AT THE CHILDREN)   And why in Apollo's name are you both dressed so very peculiarly?

SUSAN: (LOOKING AT BEAU'S RIDICULOUS GARB) You think we're dressed peculiarly!

BEAU: Why, you look like a pair of cabin boys!

LADY CHARLOTTE: And rather unruly, foreign cabin boys at that.

BEAU: Yes, from Spain or Portugal, or perhaps the lowest depths of Araby. Extremely peculiar.

SUSAN: We don't look in the least bit peculiar. I think you look peculiar!

BEAU: Me? Really? Good heavens, girl, in what way do I look peculiar?

MICHAEL: I think, sir, my sister believes your suit is a little loud.

BEAU: Loud? What can the child possibly mean?

LADY CHARLOTTE: What nonsense!   Mr Beau Brummel is the best-dressed man in London.

BEAU: Yes, I should jolly-well say I am! I think you are the rudest most preposterous two children I have seen for a very long time and I would be obliged if you would state your business then both leave my home immediately.

MICHAEL: (DIFFIDENTLY) We'd like our treasure

back, please.

BEAU: Treasure? What treasure?

SUSAN: The gold plates and goblets and jewels that you won from Lord Fairfax in a card game last night.

MICHAEL: I'm afraid, sir, that Lord Fairfax stole the treasure and had no right to wager it with you in a game of cards.

BEAU: I must be hearing things! Do you suppose I care how Fairfax came by his confounded booty?

SUSAN: But it belongs to the monks at Monckton Abbey. It was stolen first of all by Captain Blood then his idiot son stole it from him and hid it in Ireland only he forgot where ...

MICHAEL: Until it was found again by Lord Fairfax who had absolutely no right to stake it in a card game.

BEAU: Why ever not?

SUSAN: Because it did not belong to him!

BEAU: So what?

MICHAEL: Well, because it is stealing, sir and stealing is wrong.

LADY CHARLOTTE: Stealing! You say this hoard was stolen from the monks of Monckton Abbey, but where do you suppose the monks got the treasure in the first place?

SUSAN: I don't really know, I've never thought about it before.

BEAU: Precisely! How could an order of monks acquire such a treasure if it hadn't been stolen in the beginning?

MICHAEL: I can't believe that the monks stole the treasure.

LADY CHARLOTTE: Why not? How else could they have come by it? You don't think they earned it by growing cabbages or whatever they do?

BEAU: No indeed! Far more likely they extracted the booty from gullible worthies by promising them dispensations.

SUSAN: Dispensations?

BEAU: They got their gold in return for praying for the sins of ninnies who have more money than sense!

LADY CHARLOTTE: Of course what you say is absolutely true my dear, the monks have no more right to the treasure than you do.

SUSAN: (INDIGNANTLY) Well, we jolly well want it back so that we can give it to our Uncle Philip.

BEAU: And who is Uncle Philip?

MICHAEL: He's the vicar of Monckton Parish

Church.

BEAU: (RINGING A BELL FOR HIS SERVANT WHO APPEARS INSTANTLY) Another grasping Man of God! So, young sir, you can tell your Uncle from me that he can whistle for his damned treasure – it's mine and I fully intend keeping it!

LADY CHARLOTTE: Well said, Beau! Now the pair of you will leave before Mr Brummel asks Carstairs to throw you out.

SUSAN: But –

BEAU: Not another word, I've heard quite enough. Carstairs, show these two urchins the door!

(AS THE CHILDREN ARE HAULED DICONSO-LATELY FROM THE ROOM, BEAU AND LADY CHARLOTTE RESUME THEIR FORMER POSI-TIONS)

LADY CHARLOTTE: Oh my Beau!

BEAU: Oh Lady Charlotte!

(THEY CLASP EACH OTHER PASSIONATELY AND KISS)

10. EXT.BEAU'S LONDON HOUSE. STUDIO. NIGHT

(THE FOUNTAIN SPIRITS ARE LOUNGING ON EI-THER SIDE OF BEAU'S FRONT DOOR AS THE TWO CHILDREN ARE THROWN INTO THE STREET BY

CARSTAIRS)

CARSTAIRS: (BROAD COCKNEY) Now, git out of it and don't show your ugly little faces here again!

(CARSTAIRS SLAMS THE DOOR AND THE CHILDREN PERCH DISCONCERLATELY ON THE STEP)

HE-SPIRIT: That wasn't entirely successful, was it?

MICHAEL: No, I'm afraid it wasn't.

SHE-SPIRIT: You didn't really think that rogue would give you the treasure back just like that did you?

MICHAEL: He won it in a game of cards, it's not as if he had to do any work for it.

HE-SPIRIT: The boy is unutterably naïve!

SHE-SPIRIT: Incredibly naïve!

MICHAEL: I was simply trying to appeal to his better nature.

HE-SPIRIT: Ha!

SHE-SPIRIT: Beau Brummel: the greatest dandy and rascal London has ever known and the nincompoop tries appealing to his better nature!

(THE SPIRITS WANDER OFF ALONG THE ROAD LAUGHING)

MICHAEL: Hey, wait for us!

SUSAN: (WHISPERING TO MICHAEL AS THE CHILDREN HURRY AFTER THE GHOSTS) What does 'naïve' mean?

MICHAEL: I think it means simple.

Did Hédi respond passionately to your kiss?
You really do want to know bleedin' everything, don't you! There was no French kissing in those days! Not on the sets of BBC productions anyway, but yes her lips were very full and slightly parted – it was for me at least intensely erotic.

Want to hear how she describes it in her diary?
Actually, yes I would – very much.

Friday, November 24th 1967

What an extraordinary day! Finished taping Episode 3 of FoT at 7.30pm and thankfully missed the worst of the rush-hour to get home in time for Radio Three's broadcast of Peer Gynt from Manchester – Sally Fields, my friend from Rada was excellent as Solveig but some of the other playing was a little lifeless and under characterised. I almost wish I could say the same for my current job!

Had lunch with Robin in the BBC canteen and shared with him my concerns about playing this awful ghost in this horrid serial. I thought he would think I was a great idiotic twit but I needn't have worried because he was really very nice. He said he'd acted in productions of plays where the story had got under his skin and that it showed alpha emotional commitment to the role. He told me about the original serial in 1954 where he had become so engrossed in his part that he'd begun to believe that certain things in the story were actually true – mind you he was 12 at the time and I'm 25! I told him I couldn't help believing that there was something fundamentally repellent about some of the characters and that the story was weird and almost horrific in places and that I couldn't understand why no one else seemed to notice. He said I should read Mackinder's book for greater insight into the story. Not bloody likely!

The moment I have been secretly dreading for days was fine! Robin was incredibly professional all afternoon and when it came to the dreaded scene he kissed me very nicely and I was so relieved I actually thanked him afterwards! No ill effects on the emotions so far … but … but …

This is perfectly ridiculous! I absolutely refuse to admit that I am in love with Robin Glass. Dear God will I never learn? Do I want to go all through the same torment I had with Tony? What is it with me and married men? There must be something very abnormal about a woman continually setting her cap at unavailable lovers. Well, not continually – there was only Tony – but that was bad enough.

And this one's got two young children! What an appalling bitch I am! Oh, Jesus!

I'm interested in her concerns about the content and tone of 'The Fountains of Time' – which I must say I share — and the fact that she felt the need to talk to someone about it.
I'm more interested in that last bit you read out. Are you saying Hédi suddenly realised she was in love with me at the very moment she was writing about it in her diary?

Yes, absolutely.
But that is quite extraordinary! Don't you think that is quite extraordinary?

Extraordinary that she fell in love with you? It was rather on the cards, wasn't it? Or extraordinary that she realised she was in love with you as she was writing about it in her diary?
That just as she was writing how relieved she was not to be emotionally affected by my kiss she quite suddenly finds herself in love!

Isn't that the way of love – or rather sexual lust? The second you think you're safe from its clutches it grabs you by the balls and won't let go. I'd like to hear your diary entry for that same day in a moment but do tell me what you thought when she confided in you about her problems with her role.

Naturally I was sympathetic but I have to say at the time I believed her difficulties playing the She-spirit were a little exaggerated. She was taking on all these other parts brilliantly, it was only the role of the ghost that was spooking her as far as I could tell and I couldn't understand why because the role is a bit one-dimensional and rather low key. If anything, as the He-spirit I am a more sin-ister and interesting figure, the She-spirit I always felt was rather in my shadow.

You told her about some of your problems with the part of Michael in 1954 but you kept quite a lot back.

I tried to make light of the extraordinary events in the first 'Fountains of Time'. If I'd told her that after Episode 3 I'd suddenly become Michael Sum-merwood and had started to wander around the studios at Lime Grove looking for a hoard of lost treasure, apart from thinking I'd gone completely bonkers, she might have been terrified that she in turn might suddenly morph into the ghost of Lady Anne de Freece. And I certainly didn't men-tion that the old boy who'd played Old Daniel had pegged out in his underpants in her predecessor's dressing room.

No, that was probably wise. Can I hear your diary for that Friday when Hédi fell in love with you?

24/11/67

Now I'm in the shit! I simply cannot believe this

has happened! What the hell is the matter with me? I get this fabulous opportunity to really make something of my career with a starring role in a major production and now the only thing I want to do is run off with my leading lady like some playboy film star! I'm an absolute disgrace. Why couldn't the bloody BBC have persuaded Anna Lombard to play opposite me? I could have kissed her ugly mug a thousand times without the slightest possibility of falling in love.

Excuse me for interrupting, where did you keep your diaries – I mean presumably you wouldn't have wished Christine to see these entries?
In those days I had a large tin trunk at my parents' house where I kept the lease of the flat, bank statements and other important documents. I used to visit Mum and Dad every weekend so transferred any delicate stuff then. But Christine knew I kept a journal, I think she thought it was more of an appointments diary but in any case she wouldn't have been nosy enough to want to look through it while I wasn't there. Give the girl her due, she simply wasn't like that.

Jeez, I would have been.
You're a writer, biographer and professional nosy-parker, a very different animal from my ex-wife.

Fair comment. Do continue reading, Robin.

Does Hédi feel like me? She was uncharacteristic-
ally fluttery and nervous after the recording. Do I
say something or keep my trap shut for the next
three weeks and hope this is a pathetic infatuation
that will shrivel on the vine when I stop seeing
her? Would it help if I had an affair with her to
get her out of my system. Oh Gawd, I don't want
to have a hole-in-the-corner affair with Hédi Gela.
That's a bad sign: I'm getting all noble. And what
about Christine and the kids? Glass, you're an absolute bastard!'

Ain't that the truth!
Oh, charming! There I am acting like a proper
Victorian gent: all noble and self-sacrificing and
you're looking at me as if I was Casanova, Don Gio-
vanni and Errol Flynn all rolled into one!

**Sorry, Robin, apologies – of course you behaved
well — within the parameters you set for yourself, I know that, but I've read the rest of these
diaries Hédi wrote and I know what a state she
got into about you.**
What the hell can you do when these things happen? It's all down to our nascent genes and our
subconscious sex drives.

Nothing to do with me, guv!
Ok, what was I supposed to do: walk off the production, take my wife and kids to Torquay for

three weeks and let the BBC's legal department crucify me? It wouldn't have been like 1954 when old Lawrence pegged out, they couldn't have got another actor who looked a bit like me in to finish playing all those parts. They would have had to abandon the serial after episode three. I'd have never worked in television again!

No, no, you had to finish 'The Fountains of Time' I suppose.
After that third episode was televised at the start of December our ratings flew sky high, the Controller of BBC One was observed wandering around the set smirking at everyone and handing out fat contracts while those newspapers that hadn't bothered to notice us at the beginning of the serial were queuing up to write nice things about the show.

Sunday Pictorial, 3rd December, 1967

Trevor Duncan's Sunday 'Pic' of the Television Week

TV's bright new children's serial, 'The Fountains of Time' (BBC One - 5.15pm) continues this evening when the time travelling Summerwood children find themselves barricaded in the Siege of Sidney Street. High production and entertainment values have rocketed this teatime drama to the ratings' summit and the verve and style of a young cast has been top-notch. No praise can be high enough for lovely Hungarian-born, Hédi Gela (pictured above) who tackles a bewildering range of costume roles with increasing depth and élan. Last week's startling portrayal of grim, ghostly sister, Lady Anne de Freece was expertly contrasted with Beau Brummel's empty-headed consort, Lady Charlotte Wellesley, whose fabulous hair-do alone was surely worth the price of the licence fee. With Robin Glass's efficiently camp but sarcastic Regency dandy these two brilliant players make a great team and are rumoured to be signed for a BBC adaptation of Emily Bronte's 'Wuthering Heights' in the New Year.

I am at a loss to understand the criticism this six-parter has attracted from some quarters and I would suggest that over-sensitive viewers who find caustic ghosts and heaving Georgian bosoms uncomfortable viewing on a Sunday evening should employ the off-switch on their sets. After what seems to be an endless series of worthy but unimaginative Victorian classics on television such as 'Children of the New Forest', 'Lorna Doone' and 'The Water Babies', I wholeheartedly welcome this strange and compelling drama to our screens.

You must have been in quite a state of emotional turmoil that weekend. Did Christine notice anything odd about you?

I don't think so. Being a professional actor can have its uses and if I looked pre-occupied, Christine would have assumed it was just me stuck in the middle of an exceptionally demanding TV job. I had a good think over the weekend and decided I had to talk to Hédi about developments when I saw her at rehearsals for episode four on Monday morning. I half-hoped she would scream with laughter or be terribly shocked and refuse to talk to me for the rest of the production.

But she did neither of these things.
Of course she didn't. We briefly held each other's hands under a BBC canteen table and she told me that she loved me too.

She writes in her diary that you both agreed to a pact.
Yes, to have nothing to do with each other until the completion of the serial.

To put your emotions on ice – no more visits to Hédi's flat to swop classical albums.
We had to close down everything between us for the duration of the show, not to discuss anything or make any decisions or even talk personally together for the remaining three weeks of the production.

That was the pair of you being ultra-professional!
It was the only thing to do: neither of us wanted to balls up our careers and it wouldn't have been much of a grand passion that couldn't survive

three weeks without a consummation.

So were there furtive little looks and smiles?
We were actors – as well as playing our roles in the serial we also played the parts of a man and a women who didn't love each other.

Did you think the pair of you would get together at the end of your mutual abstinence?
I was never more certain of anything in my life. I knew that Hédi and I were destined to be together. You've read her diaries, you must know that, Jennifer.

She took your pact seriously: in the remaining three weeks of Hédi's life she hardly says anything about you in her diary. What she does mention is her increasing trauma with the roles she was having to perform in 'The Fountains of Time'. With the pair of you no longer speaking there was only the nightly journal left to confide in.

Tuesday, December 5th 1967

Why is everyone on this bloody production oblivious to the latent evil in that dreadful house in Sidney Street? I am aware that the building does not literally exist except in a partially reconstructed replica in Studio One at the Television Centre but somehow the original horror of that catastrophe in 1911 has also been reconstructed and permeates the set at odd intervals, usually when one is least expecting it.

This morning I was in costume as Maria Trasslonsky having a chat with one of the carpenters who'd been called in to reinforce part of the attic set and as he was rummaging around in his tool box I suddenly noticed that what I had at first perceived as being a largish teak box with brass hinges was no longer this but a shabby brown leather bag such as a workman might have used in 1911. I stepped back in astonishment and as I did so the 'carpenter' withdrew a heavy black revolver from the bag and without looking up at me proceeded to load it. I could see the open breech of the weapon and the bright brass shells as he slipped them into the chambers of the pistol. I turned round horrified to the open part of the set where the cameras and crew should be to find myself enclosed – trapped — by a broken-plastered but seemingly solid fourth wall.

I could hear the sound of gunfire from outside and shouting in the street below. I rushed to the window and found myself looking down into a perfectly real London street. I could see black-cloaked policemen with revolvers and rifles half-concealed behind walls and in house doorways staring up at me. I believed myself to be Maria Trasslonsky and knew I was going to lose my lover and my life and had only a few minutes left to live. I suddenly became quite calm, somehow knowing that what I was experiencing wasn't real. I closed my eyes and counted slowly to ten. When I opened them again and looked around I found myself back on the set with the carpenter tightening up some bolts with a wrench and telling me about his caravan in Herne Bay.

I should have been shaking with horror but the odd thing was immediately afterwards I felt elated with a feeling of absolute happiness. I could think only of the love and joy that I shall experience in two weeks' time. It's as if the evil must immediately be compensated for by a sense of positive goodness. But why is no one on this production having similar feelings? Why is this thing only happening to me?

You see the problems Hédi was experiencing, Robin?
I do now. If she was experiencing 'time-slips' or 'throw-backs' – whatever you want to call them, they were surely the result of conflicting emotions: sexual, emotional, romantic, relative to myself with the demands of immersing herself completely in so many complex roles in 'The Fountains of Time'. She was a young and relatively inexperienced actress – I have to say in the light of these diary entries that the job was probably too much for her.

You can be quite insufferable at times, Robin!
I beg your pardon?

I'm sorry but your actorly pride and theatrical professionalism are getting in the way of what most people would call common humanity. Can't you see that there's a pattern at work here?

No, I can't actually, Jennifer, but I'm sure you're going to tell me what it is.

I sure as hell am. In 1954 when you are playing the juvenile lead in a BBC adaptation of 'The Fountains of Time', you are persuaded that you have become the personification of Michael Summerwood and convince yourself that the treasure really exists and that you must find it if you are to secure romantic happiness with dream-lover, Billie Gibson. In 1967 Hédi Gela, in a BBC remake of 'The Fountains of Time' also becomes – temporarily – convinced that she too has become one or more of the story's characters. She also experiences intense sexual and romantic highs at the prospect of the serial's completion and this is the lure that keeps her going. Can't you see a connection, Robin?

But I was hypnotised by Lawrence England – a professional stage magician — to help me interpret a role I was experiencing difficulty with.

How can you be so sure of that? How do you know you were hypnotised by Lawrence England? He never told you he'd done this.

The poor old sod didn't have a chance to. If you remember he pegged out before the end of the production. I'm sure after transmission on the last day he'd have put his arm around me and laughingly confessed what he'd done.

Do you have any evidence to prove that Lawrence England hypnotised you?
What evidence could there be?

You say he'd worked one time as a stage magician but did he ever mention that his act included hypnotism?
Well, no, but apart from trawling through fifty years of old variety playbills how would one find out?

But you never bothered to find out, Robin, you merely assumed because Lawrence had performed every known act of entertainment in show business going – apart, possibly, from striptease – that he must at some time have included hypnotism among his talents.
OK, so you're saying I wasn't hypnotised at all but that both Hédi and myself were victims of some strange form of 'fluence that permeated both productions of 'The Fountains of Time'.

Ill-fated productions which both resulted in the deaths of their leading players.
Lawrence England wasn't a lead in 'The Fountains of Time', Old Daniel only really features at the beginning and the end of the story, Lawrence was a supporting player. He died of a massive heart attack during a bout of energetic fornication with

a woman young enough to be his granddaughter. Hédi Gela was killed in a car crash — you can't possibly suppose there was any connection between the two deaths.

The connection, Robin, which you refuse to see and accept is Adrian Mackinder's evil and pernicious novel, 'The Fountains of Time'.

Oh, honesty! How can you come out with such twaddle when you haven't even read the bloody book! Adrian's masterpiece has become a much-loved children's classic. For over fifty years thousands of children have enjoyed its ghostly thrills, narrative drive and racy excitement without coming to the slightest harm.

Then the problem must lie when it is adapted: there's something about recreating the scenes for real which arouses some old enchantment, no doubt placed on the book by its author, that causes evil to happen to those who perform in it.

Really, Jennifer, that's a bit over the top, isn't it? I think you must have been watching too many of my Hammer horror films in New York! You do realise that you've just described to me the main plot-line of 'Curse of the Mummy's Hand'!

SEVEN

Because it was very early in January the light began to fail at about half-past three in the afternoon and with no heating in the house it began to feel very cold in the attic. Michael pulled the piece of filthy blanket more tightly around his sister and hoped that she would continue to sleep for a little longer. The gunfire had ceased an hour ago and Michael wondered if he dared put his face up at the window to stare into the street below through one of its cracked panes. He turned round and gave the opaque square of glass a quick circular rub with his sleeve then glanced back anxiously across at Peter who had lit another cigarette and was smiling at him in the gloom.

"Please stay where you are, Michael, they may have sharp-shooters with telescopic sights trained on the window."

"I wanted to see if the soldiers and policemen had gone," said Michael, "it seems so quiet now."

"Why would they go away, Michael?" laughed Peter. "They think they have their precious rats caught in a trap and merely wait for these rats to go mad before they move in for the kill."

"But they can't want to kill me and my sister, they don't even know that we're here with you."

"That is true, but I think they would quite like to kill poor Maria and possibly, perish the thought, even myself!"

"I think they just want to question you," said Michael hopefully.

"And some questions they would think up to ask of me! Do you want those brutes to hurt Maria?"

"No, of course not, Peter; but where is Miss Trasslonsky?" Michael looked anxiously towards the stairs which led down from the attic.

"She is in the kitchen trying to make you a cup of tea. The police have cut off the gas to the house and she is attempting to boil a kettle using candles, which might, under such trying circumstances take some considerable time."

"Why don't you give yourself up, Peter, you can't possibly escape if the house is surrounded by men with guns."

"Well, you know, Michael, I have thought very hard about that course of action but I don't think I will give myself up just yet. For some reason I cannot become enthusiastic about the prospect of feeling the hangman's noose nestling about my neck, I can't possibly think why."

"You didn't mean to shoot the policeman, Peter, and anyway he might not be dead."

"He's dead all right, I got him just here!" Peter the Painter lightly touched the centre of his forehead with the tip of his finger and smiled. "I must say the policeman looked extremely astonished!"

"You shouldn't laugh at such a terrible thing," shouted Michael angrily, "what you did was unbelievably wicked!"

"Oh, the absolute certainty of youth! Everything is so clear to you my fine friend – how do you English put it? Ah, 'everything is in black and white'. There are no shades of moral ambiguity for you are there, my dear boy? But you are quite right, Michael" said Peter suddenly becoming very melancholic, "I am a very bad man indeed and you are a very foolish fellow to befriend me. But look, I'm afraid we have awoken your sister with our rather heated discussion."

Susan was sitting up and rubbing her eyes, feeling quite at a loss as to know where she was and why she was feeling so hungry, grubby and horribly cold.

"What time is it, Michael?"

"Getting on for four o'clock I should think, my watch seems to have stopped."

Peter the Painter laughed and rocked gently on a rickety bentwood chair that he had pulled from a pile of old and mostly broken furniture that was piled at one end of the attic. "You see, children, Time itself has stopped and we are lodged in this tiny bubble of stillness waiting for something very momentous to happen."

"You're waiting for it to get dark so you can make your escape," said Michael.

"Quite true, old boy, that is precisely what I mean to do. You will be relieved to see the back of me I'm sure."

"We thought you were our friend," said Susan reproachfully.

Peter looked pained: "You were certainly most friendly towards me when you believed I knew the whereabouts of some treasure for which you were searching, that is perfectly true."

"You said it was in this house and that you would help us to find it," said Michael hotly, "but you just wanted us as hostages for insurance in case your plans to rob the jeweller's shop went wrong."

"And as you so rightly intimate, Michael, it has gone wrong — everything has gone wrong, terribly, terribly wrong. And unfortunately, in spite of what you might suppose, in the present situation your value as hostages to me is not enormously great. Events have moved on from a position where the holding of two innocent – relatively innocent — children might have been useful to the cause, and I'm afraid you will have to remain here for the police to find you when they discover that I am no longer around for them to arrest."

"It was very wicked of you to lie to us about the treasure," reproached Susan fruitlessly attempting to brush some of the dust from her skirt, "you must have known that we would not have come here with you if we thought there was the slightest chance that you didn't have the treasure."

"Oh, but my dear, Susan, I did indeed have the treasure you speak of. I assure you that at one time it was certainly in my possession. Yes, indeed, many religious artefacts of gold and silver, crosses and chalices, with some age to them I would guess — nice rings with precious stones, all of these items once came most fortuitously into my hands, not I think the large bounty that you spoke to me of but a considerable booty nevertheless."

"But what did you do with it?" demanded Michael angrily.

"What do you suppose I did with it?" laughed Peter his face flaming in the half-darkness as he lit another cigarette. "Why, several weeks ago I put everything into a stout wooden box and shipped the lot to my home in Latvia. My countrymen will melt the items down or sell them to fund the revolutionary cause and feed and arm our soldiers in their fight against the enemies of communism. I can't think of a better use for such useless baubles, can you?"

"Useless baubles? But that's terrible!" cried

Susan, "you had no right to steal our treasure."

"You're treasure, Susan?"

"Well, the monks' treasure then, Uncle Philip's treasure that he could claim as treasure trove and use to renovate Monckton Manor so that people could visit the house and look at the gardens, the roses and the fountains and everything."

Peter shook his head sadly, rose from his chair and stubbed the cigarette angrily out on the wall.

"How can you compare doing up some rambling old house in the country for a greedy bourgeois priest which might just as well be pulled down and the site used for good farming land, or kept as a hospital or something useful, with the struggle of freedom fighters over those who would oppress them? You are young people and must be forgiven much because of your extreme youth but really I would have expected a little more in the way of common decency from the two of you. I cannot understand how you both look so poor but act like a prince and princess! But never mind, I hope one day you might decide that I was in the right about this particular question."

Michael put his arm around his sister and looked at Peter with a mixture of fear and a strange reluctant admiration for the man.

"But you have killed a policeman!"

"Yes, Michael, I have killed a policeman which was very wrong of me and which I very much regret. Now I will go down stairs and see how Maria is getting on with your tea. Please remain here where you will be safe for the time being and don't try looking through the window again. I have enough on my conscience without having to worry about you getting a bullet between the eyes!"

Peter found Maria sitting glumly at the kitchen table staring at a large black kettle that was resolutely refusing to boil, beneath which a single candle rather pathetically spluttered and flickered. She looked up at him and tried to smile.

"How are the children?"

"Perfectly well, Maria, Michael is in fine fettle and Susan has just woken up. Both of them and have just severely reprimanded me for my revolutionary beliefs."

"You shouldn't have involved them, Peter, they are so young."

"They involved themselves. I didn't ask them to follow me halfway across London to this hovel in Sidney Street."

"You could have told them you no longer had what they were seeking."

"That is perfectly true, but there again would they have believed a revolutionary anarchist like me? A more persistent pair of treasure seekers, I think would be very hard to find."

Maria poured the lukewarm water from the kettle into a small brown teapot and gave the tealeaves a desultory stir.

"What is going to happen to them?"

"Why nothing at all, Maria, what do you suppose could happen to them? I will shortly make my escape under cover of darkness across the gardens at the back, and the police will arrive five minutes later and all will be well."

Maria stopped pouring the tea into a cracked china mug and banged the teapot violently onto the table.

"But what is to become of me. Peter, am I to be left here for the police to arrest?"

Peter pulled out a large leather bag from a cupboard that contained the few possessions he owned and began to rummage through its contents.

"One person might escape across the gardens if they were very quick and very lucky but I fear for two people this would not be possible."

"Then you do intend to leave me here to be arrested and interrogated by the British police. Do you think they will not force me to tell them everything I know about you?"

"I do not think they will do that, Maria."

He took a packet of greaseproof paper from the holdall from which he unwrapped a large black revolver. Maria stood up quickly and clasped her hands pleadingly to her neck.

"Peter?"

"I'm sorry, Maria, you were good to me and this is a poor reward for your devotion but the

beliefs and ideals we both hold must not be com-
promised with useless sentiment."

"Peter, please, you do not know what you
are saying!"

"You must believe me, Maria, this is the
best way."

"But Peter, I love you!"

"And I love you too – I love you very much
indeed."

The shot sounded extremely loud in the
confined space of the small kitchen and Peter
stood for a moment in a daze of shock. He
breathed hard, looked down at the gun in his hand
then tucked it into the belt of his trousers. He
opened the door that led into the hallway and
stood for a minute at the bottom of the stairs listening. Then he slowly began to climb the stairs
towards the attic.

34. INT. STAIRWAY TO ATTIC. STUDIO. NIGHT

(THE CHILDREN STAND AT THE ATTIC DOOR
LOOKING FRIGHTENED AS PETER CLIMBS THE
LAST FEW STAIRS TOWARDS THEM)

MICHAEL: We thought we heard a shot!

SUSAN: Are you all right, Peter?

PETER: I'm perfectly well, Susan, now please go
back into the attic.

35. INT. ATTIC. STUDIO. NIGHT

MICHAEL: We did hear a shot, Peter, it sounded very loud as if it came from inside the house.

PETER: Please do not worry about me: I stupidly did what I told you not to do and briefly glanced out of the kitchen window. There must have been a marksman outside waiting for me to appear in his sights. He was very quick on the trigger but fortunately not quick enough.

SUSAN: But the shot sounded so loud, Peter, as if it came from inside the house.

PETER: This is an old empty building, Susan; you would expect such a loud noise to reverberate around its bare walls.

MICHAEL: Where is Maria?

PETER: Do not worry; she will be coming up shortly with your tea. Now children I would like you to help me.

MICHAEL: Yes, of course, what can we do?

PETER: Susan, there is a can of kerosene on the landing below – can you bring it to me?

SUSAN: Yes, of course, Peter, but what do you want it for?

PETER: No time for questions, Susan, please do

this for me now, and Michael, I would like you to help me pile all this furniture in the attic together.

MICHAEL: But why, I don't see . . .

PETER: Please do what I ask of you, and Susan, you are not to go downstairs, just to the landing. Do you understand?

SUSAN: Yes, Peter.

(SUSAN EXITS AS PETER AND MICHAEL BEGIN TO COLLECT PIECES OF FURNITURE INTO A HEAP AT ONE END OF THE ATTIC. WHEN SUSAN RE-APPEARS WITH A CAN OF KEROSENE PETER BEGINS TO EMPTY THE FUEL OVER THE FURNI-TURE)

MICHAEL: What are you doing?

PETER: We are going to create a small diversion that should give me time to get away.

(HE STRIKES A MATCH AND TOSSES IT INTO THE PILED FURNITURE WHICH IMMEDIATELY BEGINS TO BLAZE. PICKING UP A STOUT PIECE OF WOOD HE THEN GOES ROUND THE ATTIC SMASHING ALL OF THE WINDOWS)

SUSAN: But Peter, what about us?

(PETER STANDS SILENTLY STARING INTO THE CONFLAGRATION FOR SOME MOMENTS THEN TURNS TOWARDS THE CHILDREN WITH THE RE-VOLVER IN HIS HAND)

PETER: Don't worry, children, I shall take very good care of you.

(HE MOVES SLOWLY TOWARDS THEM AND THE CHILDREN SHRINK TERRIFIED INTO A CORNER OF THE ATTIC)

MICHAEL: You can't do this, Peter – it's all a mistake, we don't really belong here.

SUSAN: We have travelled from a different . . . it can't all end like this, it would be so unfair!

PETER: (COCKING THE PISTOL) The greatest lesson that anyone in this world can ever learn my dear Susan is that life indeed is unfair! Do not be frightened, children. I promise this will not hurt in the slightest.

(MOVING IN TO PETER THE PAINTER'S FACE, WHICH IS LIT BY THE BLAZE, HIS EXPRESSION GRADUALLY CHANGES FROM ONE OF FIRM RESOLUTION TO ABJECT TERROR. WE SEE THE CHILDREN FROM HIS POINT OF VIEW COWERING IN THE CORNER BUT NOW FLANKED PROTECTIVELY BY THE GHOSTS OF TIME. PETRIFIED PETER DROPS THE GUN AND STAGGERS BACK INTO THE BURNING FURNITURE WHICH CRASHES DOWN AND ENGULFS HIM IN A BLAZING INFERNO)

GRAMS. CLOSING MUSIC

ROLL CLOSING CREDITS

Dear God, that's such a grisly scene, Robin, no wonder it gave Hédi the heebie-jeebies. I don't know how you can possibly defend such a concoction of gratuitous horror and violence in a supposed work of children's fiction.

Well, I think I can, Jennifer. You're speaking as a citizen of a country that has spent the last hundred years polluting the world with an endless stream of dire Hollywood movies and television shows in which violent death, torture and casual brutality have been the staple ingredient. Adrian Mackinder's book is at least based on factual historical evidence and has some pretension to be a work of serious children's fiction, whereas 99% of Hollywood's output is asinine rubbish fit only for morons.

Point taken, but what I don't understand is what a conservative organization like the BBC could have been thinking of putting something like this on as family viewing for a Sunday evening in 1967.

Firstly, I think you overestimate the BBC's conservatism. At the time they were undoubtedly the leading and most innovative broadcasting organization in the world; and secondly, with seemingly endless adaptations of Charles Dickens' graphic novels regularly shown at a Sunday teatime the British public was pretty well inured to strong scenes of menace and physical violence. Good heavens, Jenny, I think I myself must have seen at least half a dozen 'Oliver Twists' on children's telly over the last fifty years and none of them shirked the moment where Bill Sykes brutally murders Nancy – a scene incidentally remarkably similar to my scene in the kitchen at Sidney Street where I murder Hédi.

Where your character, Peter the Painter murders Hédi's character, Maria Trasslonsky you mean.
Yes, yes, of course.

OK, now if you don't mind I'd prefer not to show you the diary entries for the remaining two weeks of Hédi's life because they are confused, disjointed and to me, unbearably poignant. She seems buoyed up by the prospect of being with you at the end of the shoot – although as I have said she takes great pains not even to write your name – yet at the same time she seems crushed emotionally by the pressures of performing material which was obviously deeply affecting her psyche. However there is one incident she mentions which you can help me with and that is the time she saw Adrian Mackinder's ghost in her

dressing room.

Good Lord, I'd completely forgotten all about that!

It obviously didn't affect you in quite the same way.

But it was nothing, Jennifer, honestly!

Hédi didn't seem to think so.

No, that is true now I come to remember, she made quite a song and dance about things. I thought at the time she was pushing it a bit demanding the BBC find her a new dressing room – more like the antics of a temperamental Anna Lombard than the Hédi I knew and loved. But I suppose I could have been more sympathetic. It was that idiotic pact we made, you see, it was hard to talk to Hédi about anything other than the production. I wanted to go to her and put my arms around her and tell her everything would be all right but I couldn't.

I have some testimony from other members of the cast and crew about the incident so can I hear your take on what happened?

As I remember it was two or three days before the recording of the final episode. Hédi had gone to her dressing room to try on a costume and discovered an old boy sitting bolt upright in her make-up chair. She asked him what he was doing there and when he turned round to look at her she said she immediately knew the man to be the shade of Adrian Mackinder. She screamed, dashed out and called security. When they arrived a few moments later the man had vanished. The studio and surrounds were thoroughly searched but no one was found. Even in those halcyon terrorist-free days of 1967 security at the BBC was pretty tight and we were all at a loss as to how an elderly gentleman could suddenly appear from nowhere and equally suddenly disappear again.

How did she describe the man?
Not in any great detail: tallish, thin, grey-haired, distinguished looking, sports jacket, tie and flannels. Being the only cast member to have actually met Adrian Mackinder thirteen years earlier obviously everyone turned to me to identify Hédi's description of the spook but I'm afraid I couldn't with any certainty. I suppose from what she said it could have been him. If the old chap had had egg stains on his tie I'd have thought it more likely to be the unhappy wraith of Lawrence England!

Still pining for his old flame Billie Gibson!
Yes indeed! You know there was one very odd thing about the incident: no one could find a photograph of Adrian Mackinder to show to Hédi for her to positively say that it was him. The producer, Jessie Fraser was naturally interested in the story because she scented a nice juicy morsel of publicity to presage the screening of the final episode of 'The Fountains of Time'. She contacted the Radio Times' Hulton Picture Library,

which held at that time the largest collection of photographs of famous people in the world, and they came back and said they couldn't find a single snap of Mackinder anywhere. She also drew a blank with all the newspaper and photo agency's and even Eyre and Spottiswoode, who'd published 'The Fountains of Time' in 1948 didn't have a picture of their renowned author.

But didn't the Times' obituary of Mackinder specifically state that Adrian Mackinder sent fans who wrote to him a signed photograph of himself with his Scottie dogs?

Absolutely! But as a lifelong collector of Mackinder memorabilia myself, I've never come across a photograph of the old boy either. It is very peculiar.

There must have been a photograph of him in the autobiography he published?

There was a picture on the dust wrapper of a Jacob Epstein bust of Mackinder cast in the 1930s which even his old mum wouldn't have recognized.

I suppose you're going to say the ghost in Hédi's dressing room was just another manifestation of the angst going on in her mind and perfectly explainable given the arduous shooting schedule and the amount of work the pair of you had to get through?

I don't want to sound pretentious but most people in show business, and the acting profession in particular, by reason of their calling are different from your average Joe Normals. They often have very highly strung, creative personalities and sometimes they do seem to exist on another plane from everyone else. Ghost stories in the business are legion. Every actor you've ever met will bore you with a spooky tale from their own experience if you ask them, I could tell you one or two myself. Hédi was still quite young and this was her first major television role. She'd done some stage work and a few films but she hadn't a massive amount of experience working under extreme pressure. In 1954 I'd done 'The Fountains of Time' on live television but I didn't know what I was doing half the time so all the fear and tension largely flew over my head. In 1967 although we were taping and not going out live, the tight shooting schedule hadn't much changed: two or three weeks for preparation and location filming then only a week to rehearse and tape each half-hour episode. We completed the final part of the serial on the 21st December and it was shown to nearly twenty million people just three days later. I've had a few tricky jobs in my career but I've experienced nothing more demanding on my skills and mental and physical stamina than playing in that children's serial.

So you're saying Hédi buckled under the strain?
I'm rather afraid she did.

Very well, let's move to that last day of Hédi's

life. How do you remember it?

As a ghastly, horrible day. We'd got seriously behind during the final week and we had so much to do on that Thursday and of course everything that could go wrong did go wrong: Hédi's costume didn't fit; I had to get back into that bloody fountain suit again even though the producer had promised faithfully that special effects could simply run the original tape backwards; Penelope Averell who'd played Susan like an angel in all the previous episodes decided the last episode would be a good one to have major hysterics; none of the props seemed to work; the crew were as ratty as hell because of all the overtime they were obliged to do just before Christmas; Max Cooper, the director had the world and its wife in his ear and generally everyone just wanted 'The Fountains of Time' to end.

I supposed we must have completed the final shot by about 8.30 that evening and we're all giving each other hugs and getting ready to bugger off home when in walks Hugh Greene, the Director General of the BBC with a bleedin' great cake, two dozen bottles of champagne and fifty specially invited guests for a wrap party! It had never been known before: every other BBC children's' serial had ended with a brisk handshake from the producer and, if you'd been good, a 'use you again sometime'.

You didn't feel in the mood to party!

It gets worse! I was desperate to talk to Hédi – the pact was over – I wanted to get her alone and ask her to marry me. I'd made up my mind to leave Christine, there was no other way, I couldn't live without Hédi Gela. The prospect of spending the rest of my life in a loveless marriage when the love of my life was in touching distance simply wasn't a prospect I could face.

What were your feelings in respect to Christine at this time?

Of course I felt like an absolute worm. Christine had been an excellent wife to me and a wonderful mother to our children. She'd given me no reason whatsoever to look for anyone else and as I've said, if Hédi hadn't appeared we might still have been married to this day.

So it was all Hédi's fault?

No, of course it wasn't Hédi's fault! But you can't tell when the love of your life is suddenly going to turn up can you? What do you do when it happens – pretend nothing is different? Make believe that life can just go on as normal even though your world is completely thrown out of kilter?

Perhaps you should have taken Christine and the kids to Torquay after all!

It's a platitude, but sometimes love is too strong to resist: none of the saints or moralists who ever lived ever fell in love the way I fell in love with Hédi Gela.

So the party was in full swing —
The party was in full swing. I was talking to a reporter from the 'Evening News' at one end of the studio while Hédi was chatting to the DG at the other when in walks Christine with the kids in tow.

What made her turn up suddenly like that? Had someone on the production tipped her the wink that there was something between you and Hédi?
I've no idea, I never got round to asking Christine why she should choose that particular moment to surprise me. She'd never bothered with end of shoot parties before so I guess she did appear that evening to stake her marital claim and demonstrate that I was the father of her children.

And Hédi's reaction?
She stared at Christine and in the time-honoured manner went as white as a ghost. It was quite startling to watch the colour drain from her face so quickly. Of course there was an immediate drop in the general level of conversation, and a palpable frost became apparent in the atmosphere of the studio as people began to be drawn towards the epicentre of the drama. Nothing had ever been said but I suppose the entire production team must have been aware of our feelings for each other. Here about to be enacted in Studio One was the consummation of ten weeks of suppressed innuendo and rumour.

What happened?
Hédi, still in costume dashed off the set and was out of the Television Centre in two minutes flat. Conversation resumed, as it always does as if nothing untoward had taken place and the party wound up an hour or so later. I took Christine and the kids home and crawled into bed – not the marital bed, incidentally but the one in the spare room. Christine had seen enough to decide that issues concerning myself would need to be addressed.

And that was the last time anyone saw Hédi alive?
She apparently drove straight to her flat, changed, and a few hours later jumped into her car again and was motoring along the Embankment in icy conditions close to Cleopatra's needle when the car left the road and ploughed into a tree.

And when did the police inform you of the tragedy?
They didn't. I saw it on the front page of my daily newspaper when I went down to breakfast the following morning at about 9.30.

TV STAR DIES IN CAR CRASH

Martin James
Mirror Reporter

Hungarian-born television actress, Hédi Gela was

killed when her sports car was in collision with a tree on London's Embankment in the early hours of Friday morning. Gela (25), who was thought to have died instantly, was the star of BBC One's popular Sunday drama serial, 'The Fountains of Time' which ends this weekend. The final episode of the programme was recorded only hours before her death. A BBC spokesman said the last episode would be shown as planned on Christmas Eve as a tribute to the actress. Hédi Gela's stunning looks and dramatic persona took her straight into films from drama school but public recognition came only when 'The Fountains of Time' began its serialisation five weeks ago. Jessie Fraser, producer of the serial said last night, 'Hédi's death is a terrible loss to her friends and colleagues and also to the millions of viewers who have enjoyed her wonderful performances on television. She had a brilliant future ahead of her and surely would have gone on to become one of the finest actresses of her generation.'

(Picture and Full Story, Page 5)

You must have been terribly shocked to see her death announced so baldly like that. Didn't anyone try to telephone you with the news?
We'd all got in late the night before and I took the phone off the hook so Christine and the kids could

sleep in. Later that morning a couple of reporters called at the flat but I didn't see them and Christine sent them packing.

But you did later speak to the police?
A Chief Inspector George Harris arrived the following day to interview me about Hédi's final hours.

And you subsequently went to the police station at Charing Cross and made a statement?
That's correct.

Where you were questioned for some hours and had your fingerprints taken?
You know, Jennifer, when you wrote from New York asking to interview me, I rather näively assumed you wished to quiz me about a possible sexual relationship between Hédi and myself in order to give your biography a frisson of romance that would help to propel it into the bestseller lists. I now see that you have come to my home with an altogether bigger fish to fry.

I think you left your apartment again that evening and went to see Hédi. Whether you went round to her flat or telephoned her and she picked you up in her car I'm not certain. But I believe you were in the Citroen with Hédi when it crashed. The question is, were you responsible for the death of Hédi Gela?
Why should I have wanted to do such a thing when I was in love with the girl?

When Hedi arrived home from the Television Centre that evening she had a stiff drink, a bath and then began to write the final entry in her diary.

Thursday, December 21st 1967

It's all over: my work on the television serial and my relationship with Robin Glass. Dear God, what a ghastly mess! Everything began to go wrong in the morning when there were problems with my costume. The atmosphere on set was so stifling and ominous that I escaped to my dressing room at lunchtime and cried for a good half hour. No one came in thank goodness. In the afternoon things got even worse. Everything began to go even more hideously wrong: people made stupid mistakes, the video-tape recording machines began to play up, poor little Penelope became hopelessly mixed up with her lines and all the time I felt Mackinder's eyes on me as if he was sitting behind the camera and watching everything I did. We finally got the last scene done at 8.30 pm and I had no time to get out of costume before a whole crowd of people arrived on set to throw us a party! If they had only known what a terrible production this has been I'm sure they would have had second thoughts about organising such a celebration. It's the tremendously high audience ratings of course.

If we'd filmed a normal little children's serial it would have come and gone and then been quickly forgotten. But this monster we have created with its graphic violence and blatant sexual perversion of young children has appealed to the baser instincts of a large adult audience that has been more than happy to sit in front of their television sets on a Sunday evening and take in every perverted moment —

Excuse me for interrupting, Jennifer, but that bit about the sexual perversion of young children is a bit strong isn't it?

Obviously Hédi didn't think so. If I many continue, Robin:

— and take in every perverted moment as if nothing could be more natural.

I was just about to drag myself away from the DG, who as usual was making an absolute nuisance of himself, when in walked Robin's wife accompanied by their two children! Could Robin have possibly invited them?!? Did he know about this wretched party and ask her along so that he could fling her in my face to make himself seem more desirable? Why otherwise would she just suddenly turn up like this? She looked a really nice, pleasant and friendly girl – adorable children, of course! Robin must be quite insane to want to chuck up a marriage like this for me. I realise that although Robin has been careful never to talk derogatively about Christine, I have very wrongly formed a completely mistaken impression of her as a blowsy, failed actress happy to live off his money and lounge around all day reading detective thrillers and glossy magazines. This is obviously so very wide of the mark I feel absolutely ashamed of myself.

I was so upset that I thrust my drink into the DG's hand and dashed from the studio still in full costume! It is quite incredible but the moment I left the BBC this evening I felt the weight of this terrible production lift from my shoulders like a benediction. I shall never do a television serial like this for as long as I live. And I shall never, never fall in love with my co-star again.

I still love Robin in an kind of fashion but now I know in my heart for certain that I shall neither marry or live with him, I feel much more objective about everything. I refused to come between Tony and his wife two years ago and I'm not going to break up Robin and Christine's marriage either. It's so strange: the lifting of the evil spell on 'The Fountains of Time' for me seems at the same time to have restored my emotional equilibrium and my common sense and reason. Can the two be connected in some way I wonder?

And there Robin, you have a perfectly good motive to murder Hédi. You were with her sometime early Friday morning in her car. She made it quite plain to you that she would not be running off

with you and that she had no intention of coming between you and your wife and breaking up your home. You lost your temper and grabbed at the steering wheel.

And managed to kill Hédi instantly yet walk away from the scene of the crime without a scratch. I see!

Are you going to tell me the truth, Robin?

Confess to murdering Hédi Gela? Why the hell should I?

Ease your conscience?

If my conscience hasn't needed easing for the last forty years it isn't going to require easing now.

Worried what the police might do?

If they didn't think they had enough evidence to prosecute me in 1967 they're hardly likely to bother at this late stage.

Then what's the problem about telling me?

The problem is that in giving you a nice fat juicy scoop when your biography of Hédi is published, I shall attract the opprobrium not only of my friends and colleagues in the acting profession but also of a number of fans – which you assure me I still have – on both sides of the Atlantic. And what my dear 93 year-old mum in Chislehurst is going to say doesn't bear thinking about.

It would be a scoop for me, that is certainly true, but I'm actually more interested in gaining some

justice for Hédi after all these years.
So you really do believe I did her in? Precisely what evidence do you have?

I managed to track down George Harris in a retirement home in Blackpool. He's in his eighties now but sharp as a tack. He left the police force years ago after making Chief Superintendent and still remembers the case extremely well.
What case, Jennifer? There was no bloody case.

You were in Hédi's car that night – your fingerprints were on the steering wheel.
I'd been in her Citroen before remember.

But Hédi was wearing woolen gloves when she died – it was a bitter night – and in driving she was constantly moving her gloved hands around the wheel ensuring that it should have been absolutely clean of any fingerprints. But it wasn't: four very detailed prints from your left hand were discovered at the base of the wheel, the position it should be when the car is moving in a straight line. When the car was found however the prints had moved anti-clockwise by 270 degrees – in other words the wheel had been wrenched to the left causing the car to mount the pavement and plough into a tree.
Funny way to murder someone: make the car crash while the murderer is sitting in it. Strikes me as being a bit dangerous.

I think when Hédi told you she no longer

loved you, your massive ego and conceit simply couldn't accept the rejection and you sent the car into the tree in an impulsive attempt at a murder and suicide which would bring a closure to the crisis. You wanted to kill Hédi and die yourself. Because unfortunately the car happened to be a left-hand drive model all the damage was done on Hédi's side — the driver's side — and you managed to escape without a scratch.

Sounds like a bleedin' miracle to me! Are you really going to put all this bollocks in your book?

Why shouldn't I?

Because I shall not hesitate for a moment to sue the arse off you if you do. I have supported a number of children's charities over the years and I reckon a six, or even seven-figure payout from Simon and Schuster and your good self could well be coming their way.

Of course the evidence will have to be vetted by our lawyers but I'm absolutely determined to win justice for Hédi's memory. She doesn't deserve to go down in history simply as a promising actress who also happened to be a rotten driver.

No, I agree, Jennifer, Hédi deserves more than that.

I want you to know, Robin that while I am determined to write the truth as I see it, I don't have any personal anger or desire for revenge where you're concerned. I'm incredibly grateful that

you have allowed me to come here to interview you today and I understand that, apart from the precise circumstances of Hédi's death, you have been extremely frank and forthcoming with me. I actually like you, Robin and I don't want to cause you trouble but I am a conscientious biographer I can't just sit on this and pretend it didn't happen.

Very well, I understand, Jennifer, you must do what you think is best, no hard feelings?

None at all, Robin. Now I think I'd better be getting back to London.

Please don't rush off like this, Jennifer. You must be starving; let me cook you an omelette – and I'll open a bottle of wine.

No, really that's terribly nice of you but I've taken up your entire day and I must catch the afternoon train back to Town.

There's an early evening one at 5.50. It has a dinning car and lots of room – hardly anyone ever travels on it. No chance of meeting the old guy who propositioned you – you'll have the carriage to yourself.

I don't want to appear rude and seem as though I'm dashing off just as soon as I've pumped you dry of information but I do think it best that I should leave you in peace now.

I'm sorry, Jenny; I don't see so many interesting people these days and have become rather loquacious in my old age. I must admit I really wasn't looking forward to your visit this morning – frightened of raising up old ghosts I suppose, but it hasn't been at all unpleasant. In fact you've taken me out of myself today and I thought you might like to hear the end of the story of 'The Fountains of Time'.

End of the story – of that dreadful book? For me the story ends in the early morning of the 22nd December, 1967 with Hédi's untimely and tragic death.

Hédi's story perhaps, but not mine. My life didn't stop that Christmas and if, as you say, you've found what I've had to tell you about my career to be of some interest then I really do think we should bring it up to date. You see there was a third television production of 'The Fountains of Time', five years ago, a hundred-minute television film shown on Channel 5 in which I played Old Daniel. Are you quite certain you wouldn't like to hear about it?

EIGHT

Would I be correct in assuming that Christmas in 1967 wasn't the nicest you'd ever spent?

You would. I was in an absolute state of shock over Hédi's death and it was perfectly obvious to Christine over the festive period that something had been 'going on' between us. Being the truthful, straightforward chap I am I saw no point in fudging the issue and confessed my infidelity.

But you hadn't actually been physically unfaithful to Christine, had you?

A technicality surely, Jennifer? As far as Christine was concerned I might just as well had tons of sex with Hédi, it really made no difference. The adultery be it physical, mental or emotional was transparent and she therefore asked me to quit the family home.

Far be it from me to get within a million miles of condoning rampant male philandering, but I must say in your case I think Christine's reaction does seem a little harsh.

Do you? Well, I suppose times were different then.

People are more inclined to forgive unfaithfulness these days simply because there is so much more of it about. In 1967 divorce was still a dirty word but 'affair' was an even dirtier one. I understood Christine's point of view. I didn't like the way she now saw me but she had been given ample evidence that I no longer loved her and therefore reacted in what she considered to be an appropriate way.

Surely you tried to talk her round?
I did, but the ghost of Hédi Gela seemed always to come between any attempts at reconciliation. If Hédi had been still alive Christine could have fought for me, screamed, made a gigantic fuss, issued threats and curses, pulled her hair out, pulled Hédi's hair out. But with Hédi dead and martyred there could be no contest. She knew I could never now fall out of love with Hédi Gela, and truth to tell I never have.

You were divorced quickly?
I provided grounds with a prostitute – sorry, occupation described in court as a 'model' – and before I knew it I was a single man again.

How did you like that?
Not very much. It was the swinging sixties remember and I had plenty of opportunity to party, but after everything that had happened to me I really didn't feel in the mood and in a similar way to my reaction after the Billie Gibson episode I

emotionally went into my shell a bit. I decided I would throw myself into my work and hoped that even if my love life was in a mess at least I could crack on with my career and achieve something on that front.

And you did this?

I have to say that after taping 'The Fountains of Time' my previous good fortune in the business seemed to desert me. The BBC came up with 'Wuthering Heights' as promised but with Hédi no longer around to play Cathy they searched long and hard for a replacement and at one stage even suggested using Anna Lombard of all people – can you imagine how ghastly she would have been in the part? I nipped that idea very firmly in the bud and in the end they chose a nice little girl to play the role, Toni Payne – have you heard of her?

No.

I'm not surprised, she was adequate but had nothing like the range and dynamic that Hédi would have brought to the role. To be honest I don't think I was that great either. Heathcliffe is an easy character to overplay and the way I was feeling emotionally was reflected in a performance that ran the gamut from A to Z and then went on to do another couple of alphabets.

At least you must have looked the part.

I had a lot of long black hair whose extraordinary antics in the wind and driving rain was one of the

more arresting features of my performance. After
'Wuthering', the BBC stuck me in Robert Louis
Stevenson's 'Kidnapped' as Alan Breck. That was
all right – not fabulous, but OK. My agent, Phyllis Barnes, had been trying for some time to break
me in Hollywood but it was a no-no. I was offered
parts in reasonable pictures but none were leading roles and after the huge audiences garnered by
'The Fountains of Time' we both thought it was
right to stick out for something better than being
the hero's pal which I'd already played to death in
my British films.

Then the Hammer Horrors came along.
Two scripts with lead roles appeared simultan-
eously on my desk: 'Carry on Doctor' and 'The
Blood of Frankenstein'.

You'd have been marvellous in a 'Carry on'!
Thank you, Jennifer, but I beg to differ. Anyway
Phyllis and I plumped for 'Frankie' and I went on
to do another half a dozen pictures for the Hammer boys.

Did you enjoy filming horror scripts?
They were fun to do I suppose, with plenty of
laughs on the set at Pinewood but I knew they
were crap and felt I should be doing something
better.

**And in making these movies did your conscience
trouble you at any time about the content of what
you were purveying to an audience, which I pre-**

**sume mainly consisted of impressionable teen-
agers?**

Good God, no! Why the hell should that worry me?

**You don't think movies have any effect on the
minds of their audiences?**

I sincerely hope they do otherwise I've been
wasting my time for the last fifty years. Of
course people are moved, frightened, saddened or
amused by what they see on the screen, but films
don't really change the way people think. When
I was a child I was extremely fond of the cinema
and rarely missed a visit to the Granada Cinema
in Sydenham – long pulled down to make room
for a supermarket. Week in week out I would
watch a diet of detective thrillers, gangster films
and westerns, every single one of which ended
with the hero victorious and the villain killed,
imprisoned, executed, shamed or whatever other
Nemesis the writers could concoct for him. When
this happened all the Teddy Boys, louts and teenage delinquents in the cinema would clap, whistle
and stamp their feet in happy approval. Did this
salutary weekly lesson ever persuade one of these
pimply hobbledehoys that crime didn't pay? Of
course it didn't. The yobs would go straight out
and pinch some old dear's purse or go thieving
lead from church roofs.

**Those Hammers became rather tawdry in the end
didn't they with lots of smut and explicit nudity?**

A bit of bum and tit, that's all – nothing that would

really bring a blush to granny's cheek these days. But it was true the scripts did begin to run out of ideas and some of the later Hammers do seem horrific to me now but not in the way their makers intended. However they paid for the alimony and tuition fees for the kids, and a reasonable lifestyle for myself so I wasn't in a position to complain. Unfortunately I become somewhat typed in horror roles and although I returned to do the odd interesting telly: 'Upstairs, Downstairs', 'Minder', 'Miss Marple', 'Morse', a large, unfillable hole appeared in my film CV when Hammer Films went out of business in the 1980s.

Then you did – what was it called? – 'Parsons' Patch'.

Yes, it was one of the better moves of my career. A small company, Angel Films, who I'd never heard of, sent me half a dozen scripts based on the Jack Parsons' books by Bernard Spear with the suggestion that I not only star as the eponymous 1930s Devon detective but that I also invest some money in the project, the first offer being dependant on my accepting the second. I read the treatment and decided that 'Parsons'' cosy crimes with a nice period setting might be just the ticket for some undemanding 1990s Sunday evening telly. I was in my 50s and had the necessary kindly wrinkles to carry off the role and it turned out to be a great success. I not only won my belated television audience back but I also managed to stuff a nice lot of fifty quid notes under the mattress.

And then you did some Shakespeare?
In 1997 I decided that the Great British Public had
had enough of seeing me arsing about every Sunday evening as cuddly Jack Parsons and suggested
to the scriptwriters that they devise some suit-
ably dramatic ending to the series. All they could
think of was having me drown in a disused chalk
pit trying to save the life of a small boy.

**They were getting back at you because you killed
their money cow.**
Probably. I'd done a bit of Shakespeare in rep
and on the radio and it was something I'd always wanted to revisit. I approached various pro-
moters I knew in the business but no one seemed
to think Robin Glass as Othello or King Lear in the
West End represented a money making scheme
and so I decided to go it alone. I got together a
bunch of like-minded pals, including my son and
daughter, and we formed what was in effect a rep
company for the 90s. I put most of the money in
but that was only fair – if it was successful I would
stand to take most out. We got a couple of grants
from the Greater London and Kent Councils and
started off touring Maidstone and Deptford secondary schools. Well, if you've ever seen the usual
sort of theatrical companies that tour schools you
will know what they're like.

Total balls.

You obviously have seen them. We were mustard. I directed and produced all the plays myself and I insisted that only West End standards would be good enough for those Kent and South London school children. James, my son did the lighting and Katy, then an aspiring actress, played opposite me. The kids loved us and so did their teachers. Word soon spread and parents demanded to be allowed to see our performances. A television documentary brought us to the attention of those same money moguls who had kicked me out of their offices six months earlier and someone had the bright idea that profit might be earned by doubling up performances, one for the kids in the afternoon, and one in the evening for paying parents, touring all the secondary school halls in the country that could provide a decent playing area.

So you actually made money from the Bard.
I did – and I had four marvellous years doing what I loved. Highlight of my acting career, I'd say.

Along with 'The Fountains of Time' of course.
Absolutely!

You had remarried by this time?
I married Lili Sandor at a church in Budapest in 1984.

Another Hungarian girl!
And before you ask, yes she was a Hédi clone. I don't know what I could have been thinking of but after doing a film in Germany I suddenly found

myself with some free time on my hands and on an impulse I jumped on a plane and flew to Hungary. Hédi had told me something about her homeland and I suppose it was a kind of pilgrimage or perhaps I was just seeking to lay Hédi's ghost.

And did you?

For a time. I saw Lili performing Terence Rattigan, of all people, in Hungarian at a small theatre in the sticks – she was very amusing and rather good. There was an obvious physical resemblance to Hédi and she had something of her wit and quick intelligence. I bulldozed through a romance and within weeks we were married.

Where did you live?

Lili of course wanted to live in London, as close to the bright lights as possible. I thought London was a rather boring place in the 1980s but then I suppose I was getting on a bit and becoming a tad boring myself. Anyway I put down what I thought was a huge amount of money on an apartment in Chelsea which actually turned out to be an extremely good investment. Lili tried to break into film and television over here but unlike Hédi, her English had quite an accent, which she could never manage to iron out and unfortunately opportunities for actresses with thick Hungarian accents on British television are somewhat limited. She did a few things but in the end got fed up with the business and concentrated instead on having a good time.

No children?
No, thank God! I stuck it out in London for a couple of years then I saw a property advertisement that said my hero Adrian Mackinder's cottage in Kingsbridge was up for sale and so came the parting of the ways. It was all very amicable and although we still exchange birthday and Christmas cards I haven't seen Lili since.

And have you been happy here?
Very, it was roses all the way until I became ill a couple of years ago – but that could have happened to me anywhere.

So were you actually retired from the acting profession when the offer came to play Old Daniel in the third version of 'The Fountains of Time'?
More or less, it was the year before my arthritis was diagnosed but I was relatively hearty up to then and the sort of crappy 'cameo' parts I was being offered on TV had allowed me to slip into a very welcome retirement. I was active for my age and had lots of other interests apart from show business so I wasn't desperate to do any more work.

How did you come to get the part?
Actually it's quite interesting how the offer came about. An outfit glorying in the name of Stuffed-Shirt Productions, belying their title, had been known for producing reality programmes and soft-porn sex shows for the more risqué cable and

satellite channels. Apparently some business opportunity occurred whereby they needed to rapidly increase the cultural content of their — up till that time — utterly plebeian output and so some extremely complicated deal was done with Channel 5 who consequently commissioned from Stuffed-Shirt a two hour drama which would appeal to a family audience.

And they chose to remake 'The Fountains of Time'. My God!

Now why they plumped for Adrian Mackinder's beautiful novel is something of a mystery. The producer, director, writer and the entire production team were all hired from outside Stuffed-Shirt's usual reality/porn show staff – for obvious reasons – so no-one had a great deal of contact with the company itself. There was an executive producer on the project who apparently had some tenuous connection with Stuffed-Shirt but he was never seen from day one of the shoot to the completion of the film. What person or persons within that organisation first suggested using Mackinder's novel remains a mystery.

Presumably you were chosen to play Old Daniel because you'd featured in the two previous versions?

Now that was another very odd thing. I turned up at the first production meeting expecting – if not an enormous cake complete with candles and a swift chorus of 'For He's a Jolly Good Fellow', celebrating my previous involvement – at least some comment at the fact that I'd been in 'The Fountains of Time' before and how this information might be best used for publicity purposes. But not a word was said by anyone! The meeting ended and as I walked out it suddenly dawned on me that no one in fact knew that I'd been on television in 'The Fountains of Time' before. It turned out that I'd been selected to play Old Daniel simply because I lived close to the main filming location thereby saving Stuffed-Shirt on my travelling and accommodation expenses!

Didn't you say anything to anyone?

If Stuffed-Shirt had chosen me to play in the show merely so that I would save them expenses, I wanted to see how the production was going to pan out before I offered them a ton of free publicity. If the film turned out to be a solid gold turkey then it would be best if my association with it was kept to a minimum. Obviously if the shoot turned out well I would then be in a position to supply my employers with a large favour.

What was the script like?

Excellent. It was written by Mike Stephens, who I already knew because he'd once scripted a very good episode of 'Parsons' Patch' in the 80s. Of course whereas the two television serials had three hours to tell the story, Mike had to condense a fair bit to make the 100-minute time slot. He carved away a lot of what he considered to be Mackinder's poetical irrelevances and philosophical meanderings, but he retained all the main characters and incidents in the book. The Christian subtext which previous adaptors had rigorously cut through reasons of good taste and blasphemy, Mike ignored simply because he considered it boring, but he kept the 'ghosts as aliens' story line in which was nice.

Was the script updated and given a contemporary feel?

No it wasn't. The 1967 serialisation had been updated to the sixties because the 1940s seemed very dull and dreary at the time, but Mike liked the idea of showing Mackinder's austerity-gripped post-war Britain and was very happy to set his adaptation at the time of the novel's publication in 1948. Of course 'Dream Children' looked great with the cars, ladies fashions and clipped middle-class English accents all sounding very authentic.

They changed the title!

They do these things, don't they. I can think of worse titles they might have chosen.

How did this cast compare with the 1967 one?

Not bad. Hédi's role was played by a pretty ex-Stuffed-Shirt game show hostess and my part was played by a boy-band pop singer.

Jesus!

They were OK. The director was very good with them – spent a lot of time coaching the pair how to act. The special effects in the film were superb and the photography was excellent. They'd found this palatial Elizabethan House just a few miles down the road from here, which made a very good Monckton Manor. Unlike the two studio-bound BBC serials practically everything was filmed on location, in glorious colour and in spite of my first doubts about the penny-pinching antics of Stuffed-Shirt, the production did look as though some money had been spent on it.

How did you feel playing Old Daniel?
All right. I was dreading having to play him as an ignorant old country bumpkin a la Lawrence England, which in the book he patently isn't but Baz Jordan, the director, let me do him my way. I kept the Devon accent down to a minimum and, unlike dear old Lawrence England's performance managed to avoid giving the impression that Old Daniel was permanently pissed-up on apple cider.

4.EXT.THE ROSE GARDEN. MONCKTON MANOR. DAY

MICHAEL IS ROCKING SUSAN AS SHE SQUATS PRECARIOUSLY IN A WHEELBARROW AND GENERALLY THE CHILDREN ARE MAKING THOROUGH NUISANCES OF THEMSELVES AS OLD DAN-

IEL, KNEELING BY A FLOWER BED, IS TRYING TO
WORK ON THE GARDEN

MICHAEL: Daniel?

DANIEL: Yes, Michael?

MICHAEL: May I ask you a question?

DANIEL: You may.

MICHAEL: It's about treasure.

DANIEL: I thought it might be!

MICHAEL: Just supposing Susan and I discovered
the whereabouts of a large amount of treasure:
gold and jewels, that sort of thing, and then,
through no fault of our own the treasure was
taken from us – stolen from us in fact by some
very wicked men – but we were then given the opportunity of stealing the treasure back so that we
could use it to help people, people who were more
needing and deserving of the treasure than the bad
people we were stealing it back from. Would that
be a very wrong thing to do?

SUSAN: And if we had absolutely no intention of
keeping any of the treasure for ourselves. That
couldn't possibly be a bad thing could it?

THE OLD BOY SITS UP TO EASE HIS ACHING BACK
WITH A LOOK OF COMPLETE BAFFLEMENT ON
HIS FACE

DANIEL: So where might this treasure of yours – which isn't yours, but you think it should be yours – where would that be at this moment?

MICHAEL: (FLUSTERED) We didn't say the treasure actually existed, we were asking you what we should do in case the treasure did exist.

DANIEL: If the treasure don't exist you got nothing to worry about, have you?

SUSAN: But if it did exist, Daniel, would we be allowed to pinch it back?

DANIEL: Seems to me, Michael and Susan, as if you got yourself well and truly caught on the horns of a moral dilemma.

SUSAN: A moral dilemma?

MICHAEL: It means having a choice of actions between two things both of which could be wrong.

DANIEL: Yes, and you're not allowed to do nothing either, 'cause that's wrong as well!

SUSAN: Then how can we possibly do what is right, Daniel?

DANIEL: You got to cut the Gordian Knot.

MICHAEL: The Gordian Knot, what's that?

DANIEL: Now, I'll tell you. In one of his famous campaigns, Alexander the Great arrived with his army at a city outside whose gates was a fabulous chariot that was bound together with the largest, most complicated knots that anyone had ever seen. Now the legend was that the person who found a way to untie all these knots would have the entire world delivered to him on a plate. Trouble was the knots were so big and so complicated that no one, not even a fellow as smart as Alexander the Great could undo them.

SUSAN: So what did Alexander the Great do?

DANIEL: He took out his sword and cut the knots with one swipe. That's what it means to cut the Gordian knot see: you solve the problem by using unexpected force or by doing something that no one else had thought of. Seems to me that's what you got to do with your problem.

MICHAEL: (DOUBTFULLY) I think I understand.

DANIEL: (RESUMES GARDENING) Now, if there's nothing else, children I'll get back to the job in hand.

SUSAN: There was one other thing, Daniel.

DANIEL: (MUTTERS SOMETHING UNDER HIS BREATH) And what might that be Miss Susan?

SUSAN: It's about ghosts.

DANIEL: I could see it coming! Well, what about them?

SUSAN: What I want to know is can one always be sure that ghosts always have our best interests at heart?

DANIEL: Eh?

MICHAEL: What my sister is trying to say is this: supposing one actually met a ghost and it appeared to be friendly – or sort of friendly — and helpful, could the ghost actually be relied on to do what it said it was going to do?

DANIEL: And what is it going to do?

SUSAN: (BRIGHTLY) Help us find the treasure of course!

DANIEL: What you mean the treasure you want to steal back from the wrong'uns what stole it from you in the first place?

MICHAEL: That's right!

DANIEL: And you're depending on a ghost to help you?

SUSAN: Two ghosts actually.

DANIEL: (AFTER A LONG PAUSE FOR REFLECTION) Well, if I were you I'd put the problem to the two ghosts and let them sort it out between the pair of them.

MICHAEL: Oh Daniel, now you're making fun of us!

DANIEL: Not me, Master Michael! I just sees this as a perfect example of Alexander the Great's Gordian Knot. I should think your two ghosts would be best placed to cut that old knot and solve the problem in a trice. If they're as kindly and helpful as you say they are you won't go far wrong with the pair of them.

SUSAN: Actually when I think about it I don't know if they are that kindly, do you Michael?

MICHAEL: And not that helpful either!

Now I suppose at this happy point in the story I should ask you, Robin, who died and who was spooked on this 2003 film of 'The Fountains of Time' – sorry — 'Dream Children'?
What do you mean, 'who died and who was spooked'?

In 1954 Lawrence England collapsed with a heart attack near the end of the production while you had been bewitched into believing that you were treasure hunting for real. In 1967 Hédi Gela became convinced that part of the set she was acting in really was Sidney Street and she was killed – or possibly murdered — on the final day of the shoot.
No one died on the production of 'Dream Children', and no one became convinced that the

story was real! It was a perfectly ordinary television film production: everything went extremely
smoothly; to be perfectly truthful, in my fifty
years in the business I'd be hard pressed to think of
a time when I worked with a happier set of crew
and cast. No one died, Jennifer and no one was in
any way 'spooked'.

Any ghosts?
Not one!

**So nothing in the slightest bit weird or unusual
occurred during the production of this final adaptation of 'The Fountains of Time', is that correct?**
Well, as a matter of fact . . .

**I knew it! Come on Robin, let's hear the whole
dreadful tale!**
Nothing dreadful to relate I'm afraid, Jenny but
there was one tiny odd thing that I've never been
able to explain to myself.

Here we go!
The two kids who played Susan and Michael: Shelley Fox and Ryan Holden became very intimate
during the production.

I see!
No, no, nothing like that – Good God, they were
only twelve – I meant they became best pals.
Unlike Anna Lombard and myself, who couldn't
bear to look at each other off set, Shelley and
Ryan grew very close. They were lovely children,

very talented, pleasant, polite kids but they were whisperers. As soon as the camera switched off they would be in each other's ears, giggling and whispering like best mates at the back of the classroom.

So what was wrong with that?
Nothing was wrong with it. I said they were nice kids and I was very fond of them. I did have a very small problem in that with the passing years I have grown rather deaf. It's not something one goes around blabbing about in the acting profession – it's hard enough to get work as it is without telling everyone you've gone Mutt and Jeff. I can hear perfectly well when someone is talking directly to me like you are now but it's the peripheral sounds that are sometimes hard to pick up. Poor old sods like myself can get a bit sensitive when young people talk under their breath nearby because you always think they're taking the piss out of you.

But you said Ryan and Shelley were nice kids.
They were nice kids and we got on extremely well and I'm sure they weren't at all taking the piss out of me but I'm rather ashamed to relate that my antennae would start whizzing round whenever the children began to whisper in my immediate vicinity.

You eavesdropped on what the children were saying?

Yes, I did.

How charming. And what precisely did you over-hear?
There had been a cock-up over the leasing of a cottage that was needed for a couple of scenes in the film. The owner had not been paid in advance and had taken severe umbrage with Stuffed-Shirt. At one point the producer was even observed stuffing twenty-pound notes through this guy's letterbox, but all to no avail. Never slow to take advantage of a monetary opportunity I announced that my own home, No.9 Bluebell Lane in nearby Kingsbridge, might be made available for a financial consideration.

Being a valued member of the cast you didn't feel like giving Stuffed-Shirt a freebie?
Good God, no! I haven't been in show business for fifty years without knowing that you should never give production companies anything for nothing. I rented my cottage for a day and one of my children's charities was a grand better off – that's the kind of deal that's always worth making.

Did you tell them that they were actually using Adrian Mackinder's cottage, famous author of the book of the film they were shooting?
No, I was still playing my cards close to my chest about my previous involvement in 'The Fountains of Time' and I didn't want anyone to know anything until I was ready to tell them.

So all these people were trooping in and out of your beautiful cottage –
It was murder: I don't think the lavatory stopped flushing all day. Anyway, I was taking a well-earned breather on a very warm afternoon in that very hammock you see in the garden when I over-heard Ryan and Shelley, also taking five, in conversation.

Where were they?
They were behind that privet hedge, do you see?

Sure.
It was June, 2002 and the Football World Cup was on and their talk seemed to be all about the action. I couldn't catch complete sentences, just single words and word groups so I was hearing things like, England . . . Spain . . . Germany . . . Beckham . . . Ireland . . . Penalties . . . shoot out . . . England . . . Free-kick . . . Brazil . . . Argentina . . . England . . . England this and England that. And then suddenly I realised they were talking about Lawrence England.

Lawrence England!
They were comparing my performance of Old Daniel with his.

Jesus, Robin you must have been dreaming in the garden! How could those kids have possibly known anything about Lawrence England and how he played Old Daniel in 1954?

I can assure you I wasn't dreaming, Jennifer. When I heard my name linked with Lawrence England's I nearly fell out of the hammock.

What were they saying about the pair of you?
Of course I couldn't hear properly but I gathered they thought I was much better in the part.

I'm certain you were perfectly marvellous as Old Daniel but surely you were hearing what you wanted to hear from these kids. They were talking about soccer – you began to doze off in the hammock; then they began to discuss your performance as Old Daniel, in complimentary terms, and you spliced one conversation into the other and got the impression they were talking about poor Lawrence England.
That indeed is the logical explanation but that's not how I perceived things at the time. They were talking about Lawrence as if he was still alive – as if they knew the bloke!

Did you speak to Ryan and Shelley about this?
In the first instant I was too embarrassed to confess to them that I'd eavesdropped on their conversation. In the second instant, something else occurred that afternoon – a silly, utterly stupid thing, which you will think entirely ridiculous but which gave me much pause for thought.

I hope you're not making this all up, Robin.
Thanks very much!

I'm sorry but as you might have gathered by now I'm not a great fan of ghost stories and the way you're telling this one is starting to make my flesh creep.

OK, I'll shut up about the whole bloody thing!

No, no, forgive my squeamishness and tell me for God's sake what happened.

Very well, it was a small thing but you can hunt down the cast and crew who were there and I'm sure some of them will remember the incident. After filming at my cottage had been completed we all expected to be let off for the day but the director looked at his watch and suddenly announced that there would be time for us all to troop back to the Elizabethan House that was serving as Monckton Manor so that he could squeeze in a brief couple of scenes which involved the children and the Fountain Spirits. There wasn't enough transport for everyone, so although I wasn't actually involved in the scenes I volunteered – without fee this time – to be a taxi driver. Everything went fine with no hitches until the last shot between Susan Summerwood and the lady Fountain Spirit. Shelley Fox, who was playing Susan remember, fluffed her line with the blonde bimbo who was playing the ghost and said to her in a loud voice that everyone standing around heard perfectly clearly: 'Oh cripes, I'm sorry, Hédi'.

You're putting me on, Robin! The girl said: 'Oh

cripes, I'm sorry, Hédi'?

That's right. Shelley went crimson and immediately corrected herself – you know how children become embarrassed when they call a stranger or their teacher 'mum' or 'dad' without thinking. There was a very tiny frisson of reaction on the set but then because no one had ever heard of Hédi Gela and we were all tired and just wanted to go home they quickly did a retake and Shelley's slip was seemingly forgotten.

But not by you, Robin.

Hédi had been dead for thirty-five years. As you know by then she had become largely forgotten as a film actress. There were no books about her, no television documentaries, she was not at all in the general public consciousness. I was quite certain no one on the set remembered seeing the 1967 production of 'The Fountains of Time' – if they had known about the serial they would surely have mentioned it to me. How could a twelve-year old girl suddenly not only have got hold of Hédi's Christian name but also associated it with a role she had once played?

Did you ask Shelley why she said Hédi's name?

I didn't have a chance, she was whisked off after the take and because Old Daniel wasn't required for another three weeks I didn't return to the production until the last week of the shoot. By that time I had something else to think about.

And what was that?
I got married again.

Robin!
At the ripe old age of sixty-two cupid clapped his little wings and let loose a very heavy arrow into this old heart of mine.

But that's extraordinary! In the 1954 production of 'The Fountains of Time' you fell in love with Billie Gibson, in the 1967 serial it was Hédi Gela. Who was the lucky girl in 'Dream Children'?
Carol Bennet, a very attractive lady and the costume designer on the film. We'd known and liked each other for years; when we met up again in 2002 she'd recently divorced and so I took my chance and asked her out to dinner.

And when did you marry?
The day after Shelley's little slip of the tongue. As I said there was a three-week break before I was needed again. Carol left her extremely able assistant to hold the fort and the pair of us buggered off to Los Angeles to get spliced.

But where is Carol now?
Gone to stay with her mother for a couple of days. She knew you were coming and couldn't bear to sit through all my show business stories again. She has a huge fund of them herself of course and we take great delight in boring the arses of each other during the long winter evenings. Actually it's been

a wonderful five years and we're very happy to-gether.

Is she in any way like Hédi?
Not at all; in fact if anything she's more like my first wife Christine: very down to earth and certainly not temperamental in any way.

So you've finally managed to lay Hédi's ghost?
I wouldn't exactly say that, Jennifer. I'm afraid you'll find that ghosts don't go away as easily as sometimes you might wish them to.

NINE

CHAPTER FIFTEEN
Germany to Scotland

Michael and Susan, the two Fountain Spirits and their phantom steeds waited at the edge of the wood for the aeroplane to land. It was a bright moonlit evening and the fir and pine trees cast sharp shadows along the bumpy strip of narrow grassland that stretched up towards a smaller wooded knoll. Although it was the month of May, Scottish nights in springtime are often very chilly and Susan was glad that her mother had insisted that the children take warm hats and overcoats to Devon in August. As usual the ghosts sat apart from the children. The He-spirit lay on his side close to the horses, aimlessly flicking small pebbles with his finger, while the She-spirit was fully stretched out on her back with her hands folded across her chest as if she was either fast asleep or about to be interned in a tomb.

Susan thought the wraith was merely pretending to be asleep so that she wouldn't have to

talk to the children and wondered for the hun-
dredth time why the ghosts were so standoffish
and unfriendly towards them. She turned to look
at Michael who was sitting cross-legged picking
at tuffs of grass with a rather unhappy frown on
his face. Although she was sure that the She-spirit
was only feigning sleep, Susan leant towards her
brother and whispered so that the ghost should
neither overhear nor be disturbed.

"Do cheer up, Michael aren't you excited
that the treasure will be here soon?"

Michael glanced quickly in the ghosts' direction then cupped his hand to Susan's ear. "I have
a horrible feeling, Susan, that once more the treasure will slip away from us and that we shall leave
here horribly disappointed again."

"What on earth makes you think that? The
spirits said we would find the treasure tonight
and whatever else they have said or done, they've
never actually lied to us."

"That's true but I can't believe that any
aeroplane could possible land between these trees
on such a short strip of grass like this."

"But if the ghosts said the 'plane would land
here tonight ..."

"I know that's what they said," muttered
Michael, "but the aeroplane that can land through
trees within the space of a hundred yards on
bumpy ground simply doesn't exist."

"Perhaps it will be a helicopter," said Susan

helpfully.

"This is 1941, Susan and there aren't any military helicopters yet."

"What about that funny looking machine we saw in Daddy's 'Flight Magazine', wasn't that was from the 1930s?"

"You mean an auto-gyro, but that was a tiny experimental craft that couldn't possibly fly all the way from Germany to Scotland. No, I honestly think that the ghosts have made a mistake this time. After all they are from the Sixteenth Century, what can they possibly know about aeroplanes?"

"Why don't you ask them, Michael?"

Michael pulled a face and Susan knew quite well what her brother meant. Asking the Fountain Spirits anything was not always the easiest thing to do. Even the most polite enquiry might well be met by rudeness, sarcasm or a sharp rebuke. They were definitely a very moody pair of ghosts Susan had regretfully decided, and while there was no book that she had ever read about the supernatural that had suggested some ghosts were actually jovial, good-hearted spirits, she felt disappointed that her own special ghosts had turned out to be such a surly, unfriendly pair of grumps.

"Excuse me."

The He-spirit paused in his desultory pebble flicking and scowling at Michael sat up and stretched his arms.

"Well?" he yawned, and then set about vigorously rubbing his thighs as if he could ever feel stiff and cold.

"Could you please tell us exactly where we are?"

"Haven't I told you already? We are biding at the Duke of Hamilton's estate, in Dungavel, Scotland."

"Oh...thank you."

"Oh . . . thank you," the ghost mimicked humorlessly. "The dolt is none the wiser are you, boy?"

The ghost got up and began to stamp his feet as though those phantom appendages might also benefit in an increase of blood circulation. Susan wondered what kind of supernatural blood could be passing through the spirit's veins and at what temperature the raw Scottish night would need to be to make it feel icy.

"I'm sorry, Spirit, but I've never heard of Dungavel or the Duke of Hamilton," Michael said firmly, "But you told us that an aeroplane would land here with our treasure and I'm quite certain that this strip of grass is far too short and uneven for any aircraft to land safely."

"I see!" said the Spirit with a sneer. "You know a lot about flying machines do you?"

"My father was a Sunderland Flying-boat

Captain in the war."

"And that makes you some kind of expert on aeronautics does it?"

"I might only be twelve years old but I think I would know more about modern aircraft than a Sixteenth century ghost!" retorted Michael hotly.

"Ha! I don't see how a boy who has lived for only twelve years could possibly know anything more than someone who has lived for four hundred years," the ghost boasted, "I think even my sister, who isn't the slightest bit interested in flying machines, would know more about such things than an ignorant whelp like you."
Michael looked somewhat deflated at this but Susan was suddenly inspired with the perfect riposte to the He-spirit's heavy sarcasm.

"Then perhaps your sister could tell us what sort of aeroplane we can expect to land on a piece of ground no larger than my Granny Summerwood's back garden!"

The ghost almost laughed at this and swung round to look at his sister who then suddenly spoke very quietly, without moving in the slightest or even opening those enormous brown eyes.

"The aircraft in question will be a twin-engine, two-man Messerschmitt Me110D night fighter and fighter bomber often used by the Luftwaffe for hit and run strafing raids, photographic reconnaissance and similar covert operations and if that child asks any more questions I swear I shall whip her!"

"Oh!" said Susan, and the He-spirit burst out laughing unkindly at her obvious discomfort.

"That doesn't explain," said Michael firmly, "how a twin-engine aircraft like that could possibly land in such a small space."

"Holy Saints! I never heard nor saw such a thick-skulled pair of poltroons in all my four hundred years!" cried the He-spirit stooping quickly to pick up a handful of small stones and casting them spitefully at the children.

"Oh, don't bother with them, Roger" said his sister, finally opening her eyes and sitting up, lazily stretching. "We have gone to considerable lengths to help these two ingrates find their wretched hoard of treasure and all they ever do is ask stupid questions and argue with us all the time."

"Well, I will explain to them, Anne my dear, otherwise they will bombard us with more of their asinine conundrums which will further put us both out of countenance."

The He-spirit roughly shoved Michael and Susan to the ground and strutted around them like a particularly unpleasant junior prep-school master anxious to boast about some tiny piece of useless knowledge that nobody could ever expect to know anything about.

"Now my children, have you heard of a German gentleman by the name of Rudolph Hess?"

"No" said Michael.

"No" said Susan.'

"I knew it!' cried the She-spirit triumphantly, 'Completely and utterly, dumbfoundingly ignorant!"

She too came over to stand next to her brother and the pair of them glowered menacingly over the children. "Do quickly enlighten the gormless morons, Roger, or we'll be here all night."

"I was just about to, sister dear. Now then my children, Rudolph Hess is, or was Adolf Hitler's deputy – you have heard of Adolf Hitler I suppose? Ah, I see you are familiar with the name of that personage, excellent! Rudolph Hess has on this very night of the 10th of May, 1941 unwisely decided to steal an aeroplane from the Luftwaffe, unbeknownst to the Nazi Führer, and fly to Scotland in order, he thinks, to parley peace terms with the Duke of Hamilton, whom he supposes, quite erroneously, to represent a group of British aristocrats who would like to see the war brought to an end under any circumstances whatsoever. Now as a peace offering he has brought the treasure from Monckton Manor, yes, the famous treasure that you covet, which SS soldiers discovered in 1939 hidden away in the loft of a Polish farmhouse. He knows the plate and coin are English and he supposes that such trifles are somehow going to influence the British government, who of course will refuse to have anything to do with him and lock the fool away until the end of the war. That is the end of the history lesson and that is why my dear enfants we are waiting on a cold spring night in this delightful wooded grove. Any further questions at all?"

"I have a question," said Michael.

"Well, what is it?" snapped the ghost.

"I still don't understand how the aeroplane is going to land on this tiny stretch of bumpy grass."

"Then my dear boy, perhaps you would care to glance upward into the night sky where all will be made apparent to you!"

The ghost stepped back and dramatically swept his arm towards the heavens like a circus ringmaster asking his audience to raise their eyes to the trapeze artists waiting to perform in the roof of the big top. The children looked obediently upwards but could see nothing but the inky blue sky and the even darker clouds scurrying across the face of the moon. The He-spirit held his pose theatrically but glanced nervously at his sister as if he harboured perhaps a tiny doubt that his grand effect might just possibly go wrong.

However at that moment the children caught the sound of an aeroplane whose motors were obviously not running as smoothly as they might be.

"It is a twin-engine 'plane!" shouted Michael jumping up excitedly. "I think she's in trouble!"

As the noise of the engines grew gradually louder and more distinct, a small black shape emerged from behind a cloud and began to descend rapidly towards them. Susan squinted hard at the machine then gave a cry. "It's upside down! The plane is flying upside down!"

It was true: the cockpit had been pushed back and the pilot's seat appeared to be empty.

"Deputy-Reichsführer Hess has decided a night-time landing is too difficult for him and has already baled out. I suggest you children step back some paces unless you wish to be further victims of this impulsive man's imperious folly."

The He-spirit waved the children into the shadow of the trees and gently led his sister to the edge of the grass slope. The sound of the inverted engines, starved of fuel and alternatively coughing and howling in protest became deafening as the Me 110 went into a steep dive directly towards them. Susan grabbed her brother and they both closed their eyes tightly and waited for the aeroplane to meet the ground. There was a tremendous crash and the earth shook for a second and then there was silence.

When the children opened their eyes they saw the aircraft had ploughed into the narrow strip of grass fifty feet in front of them and somehow managed to turn itself over so that it was now the right way up. The fighter-bomber had not exploded or caught fire but wispy streams of grey smoke rose from the two engine nacelles whose propellers were folded back and twisted comically out of shape as if they had been made of India rubber. The twin-finned tail section had parted company from the fuselage and a wing with a large black and white cross had folded upwards and now pointed towards the sky.

The He-spirit grinned triumphantly and clapped his hands with obvious satisfaction. "There children is your treasure-plane exactly as I promised. Perhaps you might care to think twice or even thrice before doubting the word of a de Freece in future!"

The She-spirit rubbed her arms impatiently. "Will one of you children hurry up and fetch what we have come here for. I'm beginning to feel extremely cold."

Michael, who needed no further persuading, ran over to the stricken aircraft and began to examine first the pilot's compartment then the rear passenger seat. Suddenly he produced a small canvas bag and held it aloft. Susan gave a cheer and also began to clap her hands gleefully. However the children's excitement died away very quickly when they realized how very small the bag was. Michael had no trouble carrying it back with one hand and when he placed it on the ground and sprung open the catch Susan could not help but give a cry of disappointment.

"Why, there's hardly anything in there!"

Michael upended the bag, emptied its contents onto the grass and immediately gave everyone a rapid inventory of the measly hoard. 'One small gold plate, one medium silver plate, three gold coins, four silver coins, a chalice – possibly silver, more likely tin — a small golden crucifix, a glass bead rosary, a pearl-studded prayer book, and that's the lot!'

Susan found it quite impossible to contain herself. "What an absolute swizzle!"

The She-spirit's eyes flashed menacingly. "If that girl says everything we do for her is a swizzle just once more, so help me I shall beat her black and blue!"

"But where has all the treasure gone?" pleaded Michael. "There was very much more than this when Captain Blood discovered it under the stone bridge."

"And since then," explained the He-spirit with exaggerated patience, "the hoard has gone from pillar to post and been through the hands of some of the biggest scoundrels it has been my misfortune to meet. Is it any wonder that after 400 years there has been some – what shall we say, natural wastage?"

"Natural wastage?" blurted out Michael, "why there's hardly any treasure left!"

"Certainly nothing worth bothering about," added his sister, kicking the canvas bag disconsolately. "How can we possibly give these few baubles to Uncle Philip and tell him to do

Monckton Manor up on the proceeds?"

Michael reluctantly had to agree with his sister. "Why this would hardly cover the cost of a couple of coats of paint to the outside woodwork."

"And certainly," said Susan, "a new roof would be quite out of the question."

Like his sister, Michael also gave the empty canvas satchel a kick and folded his arms across his chest in utter dejection. "We've spent night after night hunting down the treasure for the last three weeks and all we've got for out trouble is this bag of old rubbish."

"Yes," said Susan, 'I think it's all been a complete swizz-'

Before the rest of the unfortunate word could be formed on Susan's lips the She-spirit, eyes blazing furiously dealt her an enormous slap across the cheek that sent the girl reeling to the ground.

"Ingrate!"

She followed the first slap with an even harder blow to the girl's other cheek.

"Wretch!"

The spirit next grabbed Susan's hair and gave it a huge tug.

"Swizzle indeed!"

She grabbed the girl's shoulders and had started to shake them violently when Michael suddenly came to his sister's aid and charged towards the She-spirit and gave her a tremendous push. The ghost immediately turned on him and began to furiously box his ears. Desperate to defend himself against the blows, Michael threw out his hand and found a lucky target. The She-spirit reeled backwards with a shriek, tripped up on the hem of her long dress and landed howling in a heap on the grass. It was now time for the He-spirit to become involved and laughing cruelly he caught Michael by the nose and gave it a savage twist.

"How dare you accost my sister, boy! Take that for your trouble – and that!"
Michael was no match for the power of the phantom and the two great blows to his chest and stomach knocked him swiftly to the ground.

"To think," said the He-spirit, his eyes blazing with fury, "this is our reward for helping such two dreadful urchins! Then here's the end of it! Expect no more favours from us my young friends, we have served you for the last time!"

With that he quickly helped his sobbing sister up from the ground and led her to her horse. After gently raising her into the saddle he leaped astride his own white charger. "Come Anne, we will leave these whelps to consider the import of their behaviour with the vain hope that they will eventually see the error of their actions."

"But wait!" called Michael staggering up from the ground, "you can't leave us here like this!"

"Can't I indeed?" asked the spirit innocently, "and why ever not?"

"You brought us on your steeds, how are we going to get home?"

"Why not try walking?" bellowed the She-spirit unkindly.

"Don't be ridiculous!" said Susan angrily catching hold of the horse's bridle, "it's hundreds of miles from Scotland to Devon, we can't possibly walk that far."

The She-spirit bent down to slap Susan again and the girl quickly jumped back to avoid the blow. "Then you can catch a train like normal people do. Even in 1941 there must be some kind of service running between Dungavel and Monckton Halt."

"But we haven't any money," pleaded Michael.

"You have at least three gold coins in your treasure bag," scowled the He-spirit, "use some of those for goodness sake. Come Anne, we have wasted enough of our time on this pair of impudent curs."

And with that final passing shot towards the children he dug in his heels and in an instant both horses and riders were flying through the air and out of sight over the treetops. Susan began to weep bitterly and Michael put his arm around her shoulders and stood staring into the night sky after the disappearing Fountain ghosts.

"Well, I think that's a jolly rotten thing to do!" he said.

God, that's so terrible, Robin!
It's all right, Jenny, the children hitch a lift back to Devon in an army truck.

I didn't mean that! I'm referring to the horrendous images of child abuse that scene so graphically conveys.
Child abuse, are you crazy? It's just a bit of knockabout fun, that's all.

Knockabout fun? So you condone the senseless beating of children?
By two entirely fictional ghosts, why not?

The fact that the characters portrayed may be ghosts and fictional is entirely irrelevant – the beatings are shown in a highlighted, dramatic context and impressionable kids, reading the novel or watching an adaptation of it on TV, might consider them to be real enough. You think it's a great idea for children to become desensitized to images of child violence?
Of course not! As a matter of fact one of my children's charities —

I do wish you'd shut up about your children's charities, Robin! You simply refuse to accept what an evil work of literature 'The Fountains of Time' is. I can't imagine why it was published in the first place and I find it completely incredible

that three versions of this sordid tale have somehow found their way onto English television —
British television!

Whatever. And you Robin, have been in all three
adaptations. Heavens, aren't you just a little
ashamed of yourself?
Completely crestfallen.

Did no one protest when 'Dream Children' was
shown?
Actually I did receive one very forthright letter
from a gentleman in Berkshire that I kept, now
where is it? Ah, here we are!

Dear Mr. Glass,

I have never written to a famous person before but after watching your film, 'Dream Children'
on television yesterday evening I have been em-
boldened to put pen to paper. I've been an enormous fan of your acting performances on stage,
screen and television for many years: you were
quite superb for instance as Jack Parsons in 'Parsons' Patch' and when you appeared some years
ago at my daughter's school as Macbeth, my late
wife and I were both moved to silence at the end of
the play and –

OK Robin, never mind the endorsement of your
acting talents, what does the guy have to say

about 'Dream Children'?

Oh right, I was just coming to that, now where were we?

I therefore looked forward with considerable interest and excitement to your performance on television last night. I cannot begin to tell you what a horrific disappointment 'Dream Children' turned out to be. I find it difficult to imagine what persuaded an actor of your accomplishment and repute to appear in such a shocking farrago of wicked nonsense.

Right!

That you could have aided and abetted such scenes of sexual license and physical abuse of young children and permitted such crimes to be paraded on TV in the name of family entertainment is quite beyond my understanding or, I would have thought the understanding of any sane person.

Absolutely!

Indeed I was so upset yesterday evening that if I had not been physically restrained by several of the warders I would certainly have wrenched the TV from the wall.

What's this?

Signed,

George Herbert Mansfield,
Longshot Asylum for the Criminally Insane.

I really don't find your pathetic attempt at humour to be the slightest bit funny, Robin.
Oh do lighten up, for God's sake, Jennifer! If you could only see your face. You've somehow persuaded yourself that a rattling good yarn for children by Adrian Mackinder – which you haven't read — is the work of the devil.

You have persuaded me of this, Robin. Reading these extracts from the book and television scripts you make them sound like the works of the Marquis de Sade.
Well, I'm sorry but that's just my dramatic vocal style and actorly manner. I do apologise, I'm a pathetic old ham and I simply can't help putting on a show for my visitor. I'll tone it down from now on, promise.

I'm tired Robin and I really don't think I want to hear any more of this godawful story. Do you mind if I get my things together and head back to London?
Of course not, Jennifer. I'll get the car and give you a lift to the station. Can I tempt you with a drink before you go? You look as though you could do with some colour putting back in your cheeks.

Do I really?

At the moment you look the spit of Lady Anne de Freece on a bad day.

Oh, don't say that! Yes, a drink would be very nice. Would you have such a thing as a glass of Scotch with a little ice?
Coming right up!

I'm sorry about getting so phased out and wacky, Robin – it's been a long day.
Don't mention it, Jennifer and I'm sorry about that awful gag with the letter, it was quite unforgivable of me. Here you go!

That's fine, cheers!
Actually I did get a very nice letter after 'Dream Children' was televised from a lady called Elaine MacFadden who turned out to be Adrian Mackinder's great niece.

God, really?
Against my better judgment I had finally confessed to the publicity person from Stuffed-Shirt Productions of my previous involvement with 'The Fountains of Time' and far from getting a lovely spread in one of the posh Sunday Magazine Supplements I ended up in one of the Satellite TV guides in a 'Where are they now?' article.

Oh no!
It was dreadful: pictures of me as Michael in 1954, and The Fountain Spirit in 1967 and then a photograph of me got up as Daniel looking like Old

Father Time. The feature mentioned that I was now living in the author's cottage in Devon and Mackinder's great niece remembered the address and wrote to me. I have her letter here somewhere, would you care to..?

I'd love you to read me Adrian Mackinder's niece's letter, Robin.

24, Torrance Street,
Edinburgh.

17th March, 2003

Dear Robin Glass,

A friend, knowing that I was related to the writer Adrian Mackinder, has shown me the article about you in the 'TV Week' and I was most interested to read about your life and watch the excellent film you made of my Great Uncle's book (why did they change the title???) I viewed your performance with enormous pleasure and thought it far superior to both 1954 and 1967 television 'Old Daniels'. You made him into a real flesh and blood person and not the daft comic rustic usually portrayed. I remember my uncle being highly critical of the old fellow they had in 1954, whose name I can't recall, and reading that you now live in Adrian Mackinder's cottage in Kingsbridge brought a flood of happy memories back to me.

In the early 1950s my parents owned a house on the river Dart and they often took me to visit 'Uncle Adrian' in his beautiful Kingsbridge cottage. He was considered to be quite a celebrity in the family and the fact that he never used his fame to put on airs was considered to be only correct and proper by my rather Calvinistic parents. He'd never talk about his work without you asking him first and wouldn't have dreamed of boasting about the sales of his books or anything vulgar like that!

I was ten years old in 1954 and I remember visiting him with my parents one Sunday afternoon when 'The Fountains of Time' was being televised. It was very funny because I had been following all the episodes of the serial without the faintest idea of my Uncle's involvement in the story and my dear parents who hadn't seen him for ages were talking ten to the dozen and it seemed that I would never get home in time to watch the final episode of my favourite programme.

Uncle Adrian had a television set in the corner of his sitting room. It was one of those lovely consol models on casters with polished walnut doors that folded across the screen when it wasn't in use, but I was much too shy to ask Great Uncle Adrian if I might be allowed to watch Children's Television and I thought those doors would remain folded against me forever! Of course I never realized that he too must have been desperate to watch the serial he'd written but he was far too polite to shut my parents up and just switch on the set.

Then the miracle happened! There was just two minutes to go before the serial started and I was squirming in my seat with annoyance and frustration, picturing myself at school on Monday morning asking my friends what exciting things had happened to Michael and Susan in the story, when my father idly enquired what Adrian was writing at the moment and the old fellow beamed and said the magic words:

'As a matter of fact . . .'

In a trice the television was wheeled out of its corner, the doors unfolded and the set switched on. I curled up on the settee next to my Uncle and it was quite marvellous because he gave a discrete but absolutely fascinating running commentary on the episode. I've told you what he thought about Old Daniel but he said some lovely things about your performance as Michael Summerwood. He told us how he'd been introduced to you at a rehearsal and how you shook his hand very firmly and said his book was the best children's book ever written and could Great Uncle hurry up and write a sequel!

Adrian watched the episode very carefully and would take great delight in pointing out little subtleties he perceived in the cast's performances. There was a scene where you attack one of the Fountain Spirits and he said, 'Look how the boy's eyes blaze with courage – that's being, not acting!' And when you were being tortured by the female Nazi spy, it was quite extraordinary how my Uncle suddenly became very angry and upset; his face went a bright shade of red and he rose from the settee and cried out, 'Leave the boy alone, leave him alone, you dreadful swine!' I think my parents must have been extraordinarily shocked and embarrassed by such behaviour from their elderly relative but it had the most profound affect on me because, like Uncle Adrian I became completely engrossed in the scene and I couldn't bear to see that awful Nazi woman hurting you.

I'm so pleased that you are now living at 9 Bluebell Lane; it seems to bring everything around in a circle. The last time I visited your home was in 1966 when Great Uncle Adrian was obviously dying. My parents had by that time returned to live in Scotland but I'd remained in Devon to finish my nursing training in Exeter and when they telephoned me to say that Uncle was not expected to live for much longer and could I pop in to see him I was very happy to go. I remember that day very well: it was a beautiful afternoon in early spring and Uncle was lying in bed and obviously very ill but quite alert. He recognized me at once and seemed very pleased to see me. I think he had become something of a recluse in his later years and I had been a little anxious about what sort of reception I would receive but Adrian was kindness itself.

I wanted to tell him how much pleasure his novels had given me over the years because I know authors like that kind of thing, but he waved my compliments away, he was no longer interested in literature, all that was in the past, he didn't want to talk about it. I knew his father had been a churchman and that he had brought up Adrian to be very religious and in fact most of his novels have some kind of Christian context. Being then a practicing believer myself I had thought to bring him a prayer book as a small gift but I was very shocked when my Great Uncle thanked me but announced that he had entirely given up his faith.

The odd thing was that this did not make me feel at all anxious or gloomy for him. He told me that he was very pleased to have finally shed the shackles of religious enslavement and that he was greatly looking forward to what he called, 'the alternative'. I asked him what this 'alternative' might be and he smiled and said he wasn't allowed to tell me. It was extremely puzzling but as I sat there holding his hand with the spring sunshine streaming through the window the sense of goodness, oneness and sheer happiness in the old man's bedroom was almost overpowering.

Since then I have attended many deathbeds and witnessed many kinds of passing but never again have I experienced such a powerful atmosphere of beatification in a person's final hours. I left the cottage floating on a cloud and when I heard that Adrian had died during the night it was impossible to feel sorry, only intensely grateful that he had moved to his death in such a magnificent manner.

I seemed to have wandered a long way from sending you a simple fan letter! I did want you to know how much I enjoyed your performance the other evening and to tell you that the author of 'The Fountains of Time' appreciated what you achieved as Michael in 1954 and if he could have watched 'Dream Children' how much he would have enjoyed your lovely performance as 'Old Daniel'.

Yours very sincerely,
Elaine MacFadden

That's an incredible letter, Robin!
I thought so. Nice woman.

But don't you see how it throws an entirely new light on Adrian Mackinder?
Does it?

Of course! There was I cursing the guy for writing such an abominable novel as 'The Fountains of Time' and here in this letter we discover he was as much a victim of its evil atmosphere as anyone else.
How do you make that out?

Elaine MacFadden explains in her letter how Adrian was sucked into the story as they watched it on television. He began to believe the characters and situations were for real just as you and Hédi did. On his deathbed he experienced the same kind of high as you felt in your love for Billie Gibson and Hédi felt in her love for you. It wasn't Adrian Mackinder who was responsible for the extraordinary happenings connected with the novel, it was the book itself!

Don't see how you can detach Adrian from his own novel – he wrote it didn't he?

Yes, but works of art assume a life of their own when they leave their creators. Someone once said that Charles Dickens' works are more intelligent than he was, and it's true! Look Robin, many great artists, writers and musicians, have said how they believed their creativity came from some kind of unknown source. Schubert said he felt he was a 'conduit' for his music: simply a channel through which his works came about. Mozart thought all his music had already been composed and was waiting in the ether somewhere, all he had to do was try to remember it as accurately as possible and write it down. Adrian Mackinder was the 'conduit' for 'The Fountains of Time', he merely transcribed what was given to him and was not responsible for its content. Don't you think it extraordinary that a hack children's writer like Mackinder should suddenly

have burst forth with a work like 'The Fountains of Time'?
It's certainly true that none of his other works come close to being as passionate or interesting as 'The Fountains of Time'. I always thought of him as being a bit of a one-hit-wonder.

This was the book he had to write – or was made to write.
By whom?

Who knows? He spoke to Elaine MacFadden of 'the alternative' on his deathbed but refused to say what this was. Perhaps he finally came to understand the power that had possessed him whilst he was writing 'The Fountains of Time'. This same power made you believe the Fountain Treasure was real in 1954 and that Billie Gibson would come and live with you in your parents' home in South London. It made you fall in love with Hédi in 1967, and Hédi fall in love with you and it made her believe that part of the set constructed in the Television Centre was actually a real house in Sidney Street in 1911. Let's hear the rest of the story!
What story?

'The Fountains of Time' of course: the part where Michael is tortured by the Nazis.
You've recovered your composure then, I thought you wanted to go back to London.

Now we've eliminated Adrian Mackinder from

the equation we're left with the pure story itself. Now I know my enemy I can see what I'm up against.

If you're sure . . .

I'm sure, bring it on! It's not that I haven't enjoyed hearing you read to me, Robin but you must have a tape or DVD of 'Dream Children' somewhere, can't we watch that?

No problem!

TEN

'This is BBC One. We present the final episode of 'The Fountains of Time' in remembrance of the actress, Hédi Gela who sadly lost her life on the evening of this her final performance. The programme contains scenes which may be unsuitable for young children or those viewers of a nervous disposition.'

'The Fountains of Time'

Episode six:
The Beginning and the End of Time

Pause this just a minute, Robin please and tell me what the fuck we're watching.
I was planning to keep it as surprise for you. It's the last episode of the 1967 serial.

But you said the BBC had wiped the tape in the early 1970s.
Which is what the penny-pinching vandals did. Fortunately, because 'The Fountains of Time' was

so incredibly popular the serial was sold abroad, mainly to British Commonwealth countries like Australia, Canada and New Zealand. After transmission the tapes were either returned to the Corporation to be reused or wiped in situ.

So where the hell did this tape come from?
Like a lot of bored elderly men I enjoy trawling the internet and one afternoon I was going through the television memorabilia section on eBay – embarrassingly searching for anything that might pertain to my varied and interesting film and television career — and to my intense astonishment and delight I found all six episodes of the 1967 'The Fountains of Time' on six reels of two-inch videotape offered for auction.

My God!
They had been used to transmit the serial in New Zealand in 1968 and while the BBC was negligently wiping their tapes as fast as they could clap them into the erasing machines, Television New Zealand had put theirs on a shelf somewhere and forgotten all about them. How they came to end up on an internet auction site forty years later I neither knew nor cared. The starting price for the item was £99.99 and I was so anxious to secure the tapes that I whacked down a bid of £10,000.

Holy Mother, and you won them, Robin!
They came in at £158, which wasn't so good for the old ego but I was none the less extremely

pleased with my bargain. The tapes arrived by air-mail five tremulous days later and I got an old pal at the Beeb to transcribe them to DVD for me. The sound and picture quality as you can see is excellent.

But this is a fantastic and major find, Robin! To have all six episodes of 'The Fountains of Time' with you and Hédi at your peak when we thought they been lost forever is simply wonderful.
I'm very pleased that I've managed to surprise you with my little discovery.

Surprise isn't the word, Robin, I'm absolutely dumfounded and completely delighted! Can I ask you what you hoped to do with such a treasure?
I contacted the BBC in the first place and told them what I had discovered. Needless to say they were amazingly uninterested in the re-emergence of their once famous children's serial after so long. Because it was shot way back in 1967 in glorious black and white and without any 'stars' in it, they now considered the tapes to have no commercial value whatsoever and so I made a quite small ex gratia payment to them and became the proud owner of the tapes and their entire copyright. I'd been thinking for some time about presenting the serial to the British Film Institute but when you sent me your letter I thought a first biography of Hédi would be a perfect place for a DVD of 'The Fountains of Time'. Some books do have DVDs stuck in the back of them don't they? Is this some-

thing that you and your publishers would consider for 'Undying Flame' or am I presuming too much?

You're not presuming at all, Robin, that would be an absolutely marvellous publishing ploy! I mean we intended to illustrate Hédi's last piece of work with some black and white stills provided by the BBC but it would be stupendous to actually include the whole serial as a DVD with the book. Would you want an awful lot of money from Simon and Schuster for the rights?

Any money will go to charity so I'm perfectly happy to allow you to negotiate with your publishers on my behalf.

That's extremely generous of you Robin, and now you've made me feel like a complete and utter bitch.

But why?

Because of what I intend to write in my book about Hédi and your final hours. I must tell the truth as I see it, Robin, you do understand that don't you? I've got my faults as a writer and as a person, I'm very aware of what they might be, but I couldn't publish 'Undying Flame' and leave out the most important piece of information I've discovered about how Hédi met her death, you wouldn't expect me to would you?

Of course not, Jennifer. As I've already said you must write it how you see it. I have unchiverously threatened you and your publishers with a million dollar libel case but I honestly don't think things will come to that.

You mean you're not going to sue the arse off me after all?

Shall we watch the episode with Hédi and me as a pair of nasty Nazi spies?

Oh, please, yes! Was this all taped on that last dreadful day in December when Hedi died?

It was, and you can imagine what incredible memories it brings back to me!

1. INT. LOUNGE/MONCKTON MANOR. STUDIO. NIGHT

(IT IS MAY, 1941 AND MONCKTON MANOR HAS BEEN CLOSED FOR SOME TIME BECAUSE OF THE WAR. THE ROOM IS QUITE BARE WITH THE REMAINING PIECES OF FURNITURE APART FROM TWO CHAIRS COVERED WITH DUSTSHEETS AND THE ODD TEA-CHEST VISIBLE. THE ELECTRICITY HAS APPARENTLY BEEN CUT OFF BECAUSE THE ROOM IS ILLUMINATED BY HALF A DOZEN CANDLESTICKS. SUSAN IS BEING HELD TIGHTLY ON OTTO WEISS'S LAP AND MICHAEL IS TIED TO A CHAIR IN THE MIDDLE OF THE ROOM WHERE FRAULINE HELGA GERDES IS LEANING OVER HIM WITH HER HANDS RESTING ON HIS SHOULDERS AND HER FACE ALMOST TOUCHING HIS CHEEK)

MICHAEL: I've told you we haven't got what you're looking for!

GERDES: And I've told you, Michael that I don't believe you! So we can either gainsay each other's denials as a very boring game or you can tell me the truth. Or I can quite seriously hurt you. Now how would you like to proceed?

SUSAN: (TRYING TO STRUGGLE FROM WEISS'S LAP BUT EASILY RESTRAINED) Leave him alone, you hateful, vile witch!

WEISS: (LAUGHING) Now then, little girl you must remember your manners or I shall need to spank you rather severely.

MICHAEL: Lay a finger on my sister and I'll kill you!

WEISS: Oh, now I am – how do you say? – really quaking in my boots! (HE GIVES SUSAN A HARD SLAP ON HER LEG) There! What are you going to do about that, Michael?

GERDES: (GRABBING MICHAEL'S FACE AND THRUSTING IT UPWARD INTO HER'S) You know, Herr Weiss, I rather think Michael has decided what he wants to do and unfortunately we shall be obliged to accommodate him. Let me have your candlestick, please.

WEISS: Ah, most certainly, Frauline Gerdes!

(STILL PINNING SUSAN WITH ONE ARM HE TAKES A CANDLESTICK FROM A NEARBY TABLE AND IS ABOUT TO PASS IT TO GERDES THEN ALMOST AS AN AFTERTHOUGHT DRAWS THE LIGHTED CANDLE SLOWLY ACROSS SUSAN'S FACE)

GERDES: An excellent idea but I do not think such a solution will be at all necessary.

(SHE TAKES THE CANDLE FROM WEISS THEN MOVES THE FLAME ACROSS MICHAEL'S BARE FOOT)

SUSAN: (STRUGGLING IMPOTENTLY) Leave him alone! Leave him alone!

GERDES: I do not want to hurt your brother, my dear but I'm afraid we do rather need to loosen his somewhat reluctant tongue. Now Michael, are you going to tell me where you put the canvas bag that you stole from the traitor Hess's aeroplane?

MICHAEL: I told you, we threw it away!

GERDES: Together with the secret war plans Hess intended to barter for his miserable freedom?

MICHAEL: There were no secret plans, just some old religious relics and a few coins.

GERDES: Do you suppose the traitor flew eight hundred miles in a stolen aircraft merely to bring Winston Churchill a bag of religious relics?

(SHE MOVES THE CANDLE'S FLAME ACROSS MICHAEL'S BARE FOOT ONCE MORE AND HE SCREAMS)

Do you think I'm such a fool, Michael?

(SHE BURNS HIM AGAIN)

Do you think I have come with Herr Weiss all this way to England by submarine at some considerable personal risk to our safety to take back a bag of worthless trinkets?

(SHE BURNS HIM ONCE MORE)

Be reasonable please, Michael, you don't have to be so brave. You are a good boy and no one will think any the less of you if you tell me what I want to know.

MICHAEL: I don't know, I don't know!

SUSAN: I'll tell you! Please don't hurt him any more!

WEISS: Speak very quickly, Susan, come along tell us at once.

SUSAN: We buried the bag in the rose garden beside the fountain.

MICHAEL: She's lying; we threw it away like I told you.

GERDES: We will take a look I think, and if Susan

has been telling untruths I shall allow Herr Weiss to punish her as he sees fit, which I do not think will be at all pleasant for either of you. (TO WEISS) We'll take them with us so they can show us exactly where the bag is buried.

2. EXT. ROSE GARDEN. STUDIO. NIGHT

(GERDES STRIDES BRISKLY TOWARDS THE FOUNTAIN WITH A SPADE WHILE WEISS FOLLOWS DRAGGING THE CHILDREN BY THEIR COLLARS)

GERDES: Now, Susan, the correct position please.

SUSAN: (POINTING TO THE BASE OF THE FOUNTAIN'S WALL) We buried the bag there!

MICHAEL: You're wasting your time, she's lying – she's just trying to protect me.

GERDES: Very possibly, Michael, but then I think Susan fully understands the consequences if foolishly this is what she has done.

(AS SHE BEGINS TO DIG VIGOROUSLY AT THE BASE OF THE FOUNTAIN MICHAEL WHISPERS TO SUSAN)

MICHAEL: You know the bag isn't there!

SUSAN: I couldn't bear to see her torturing you, Michael. We must pray to the Fountain Spirits and hope they will come and save us again!

MICHAEL: They won't come, Susan – they hate us

now.

WEISS: What's all this whispering about! You think I'm deaf and can't hear you? Hey, Frauline Gerdes, the children think they will be saved by praying to spirits of the fountain!

(THE EARTH IS SOFT AND GERDES HAS ALREADY DUG QUITE A DEEP HOLE. SHE PAUSES BRIEFLY AND SMILES WICKEDLY AT THE CHILDREN)

GERDES: Pray as much as you wish, children. I think another two minutes' digging will persuade me that I'm wasting my time and then certainly you will need every single one of those prayers.

SUSAN: (CLOSING HER EYES IMPLORINGLY) Please, please help us, She-spirit. I'm sorry I was so rude to you and asked you so many idiotic questions. I promise if you help us now I'll never ever ask you another question again.

MICHAEL: And He-spirit I'm really sorry I tried to fight you and that I knocked your sister down but I was only trying to protect Susan and I promise never to do anything to hurt you in any way again.

GERDES: Ah ha! What have we here?

(STANDING IN THE HOLE SHE BENDS DOWN TO PICK UP AN OLD BOOT)

WEISS: Nothing there! We've been wasting our time, Frauline Gerdes.

GERDES: (CLIMBING OUT OF THE PIT AND BRUSHING HERSELF DOWN) I'm rather afraid it looks that way, Herr Weiss. Take the girl back to the house and give her a beating – and you need not spare her!

MICHAEL: (STRUGGLING FREE AND FLINGING HIMSELF AT FRAULINE GERDES) I'll kill you first!

(GERDES FALLS BACK INTO THE HOLE AND THERE IS A HORRIBLE UNEARTHLY SOUND AS THE FOUNTAIN'S WALL SUDDENLY GIVES WAY, WATER CASCADES ON TOP OF HER AND GREAT CLOUDS OF SMOKE BEGIN TO ISSUE FROM THE TWO STATUES. GERDES SCREAMS ARE ECHOED AND MULTIPLIED BY THE HOWL OF STEAM AND THE CRASH AS THE WATER ENGULFS HER. THE CHILDREN LOOK ON EXCITEDLY AS THE SMOKE CLEARS TO REVEAL THE FOUNTAIN SPIRITS)

WEISS: Dear God in Heaven!

(TERRIFIED HE RELEASES HIS HOLD ON SUSAN AND STAGGERING BACKWARDS HE TAKES A LUGER FROM HIS POCKET AND AIMS IT AT THE GHOSTS)

WEISS: Stand back! Don't come near me!
(THE SHE-SPIRIT WALKS SLOWLY TOWARDS HIM AND WEISS BEGINS TO FIRE OFF ROUNDS AT HER WITH ABSOLUTELY NO EFFECT. SHE GRIPS HIM AROUND THE THROAT ONE HAND AND WITH ENORMOUS STRENGTH BRINGS HIM TO HIS

KNEES AND CHOKES HIM TO DEATH)

HE-SPIRIT: (PUTTING HIS ARMS AROUND THE CHILDREN) Michael and Susan, how very pleasant to see you again!

That was a fabulous scene! You and Hédi were just out of this world, Robin, tremendous perform-ances!
Thanks very much! Not too gory for you?

Not at all, very mild given the circumstances.
You didn't find our Nazis a little too sadistic?

It was perfectly acceptable, Robin.
No unpleasant sexual connotations with the chil-dren that could be objected to?

Certainly not, I thought it was all extremely well done and the picture and sound quality is sim-ply fantastic! I can't thank you enough for letting me have the tape of this serial for my biography, Robin. As I was watching it suddenly struck me that I absolutely must change the title. I've al-ways suspected that 'Undying Flame' is crap idea for the book, 'The Fountains of Time' would be infinitely better. Do you like the suggestion and do you think anyone will mind if I pinch Adrian Mackinder's title?
He's been dead and forgotten for a long time so I can't see that anyone would object. Will you be placing more emphasis in your biography on

Hédi's final role now you've seen something of the quality of her performance?

Absolutely. Before I saw this I believed the few films she made in France would be her memorial but now it just has to be 'The Fountains of Time' that my book will concentrate on. It's funny but I wasn't really looking forward to coming here to interview you today.
Why ever not?

I knew nothing about 'The Fountains of Time' and not much more about you. My interest was strictly confined to your relationship with Hédi and the manner in which she died. I thought you'd be an old theatrical windbag who'd bore the hell out of me –
But I am, and I have, Jenny!

You're not in the least bit boring, Robin and I've been very informed and entertained by what you've had to say. It's quite incredible how my feelings about 'The Fountains of Time' have changed. I'd been thinking Adrian Mackinder's book was some kind of beefed up M.R.James' ghost story – or even one of your delicious Hammer Horrors, but now I see it as quite a different kind of novel: the sort of typical humanist British morality story like The Water Babies or even Treasure Island.
Did I tell you I once played Ben Gunn in panto at Scarborough?

15. EXT. THE ROSE GARDEN. STUDIO. DAY

(OLD DANIEL IS STANDING WITH THE CHILDREN, SCRATCHING HIS HEAD AND GAZING AT THE EMPTY FOUNTAIN'S BOWL WHICH IS STILL ISSUING A DRIBBLE OF WATER)

OLD DANIEL: Well I ain't never seen no mole or badger what could dig a big hole like that!

SUSAN: We told you, Daniel: Frauline Gerdes, the evil German spy dug the hole when she was looking for the secret plans!

MICHAEL: And I pushed her into the pit and the fountain's wall collapsed on top of her!

SUSAN: And then the Fountain Spirits came and rescued us from that awful man, Weiss, who was going to beat me!

OLD DANIEL: Maybe it's a bit of subsidence, what with all those idiots in the past digging for treasure in the rose garden it's no wonder the fountain's lost her foundations.

MICHAEL: You're not listening to a word we say, Daniel!

SUSAN: We've told you about our incredible adventure and you simply won't believe us!

OLD DANIEL: Yeah! Nazi spies, Fountain Ghosts,

secret plans, lost treasure, found treasure, lost treasure again. Incredible is certainly the word I'd use.

MICHAEL: I think you should be ashamed of yourself for doubting what we tell you.

OLD DANIEL: Oh dear!

SUSAN: You've seen the gap in the fountain's wall and all you can say is you think a mole or badger has caused it. I tell you last night the most dreadful witch of a women anyone ever met was lying dead beneath that marble!

OLD DANIEL: So where is she now then?

SUSAN: Pardon?

OLD DANIEL: Where's the old witch what young Michael here pushed down the hole – where is she at this present moment?

MICHAEL: Oh, the Fountain Spirits made both of the dead Nazis disappear!

OLD DANIEL: 'Course I understand! Well, I'd better go see your Uncle and get him to phone through to the builder, see if he can take a look at it. Cost a pretty penny to repair the old fountain, set her up proper again. Wouldn't be at all surprised if your Uncle decides not to bother.

SUSAN: Not bother? Not get the fountain going again?

OLD DANIEL: That's right, stick up a nice little ornamental sundial instead, that's what I'd do.

MICHAEL: A sundial, instead of the Fountains of Time?

OLD DANIEL: Be a darn sight cheaper.

SUSAN: But we can pay for it with the treasure, Michael! Those gold coins and plates and things must be worth a few hundred pounds!

MICHAEL: Of course! We'll get the treasure and take it to Uncle Philip at once, come on!

(THE CHILDREN DASH OFF LEAVING OLD DANIEL STILL STARING DOWN INTO THE HOLE AND SCRATCHING HIS HEAD)

That old guy playing Daniel in 1967's pretty hammy. Could we take a look at how you played him in 2002?
Unfortunately we can't. 'Dream Children' hasn't, as far as I'm aware, been released on video or DVD. It wasn't that much of a success you know. Stuffed-Shirt were very disappointed at the programme's low ratings and quickly fled back to the safety of producing porn and reality shows.

But you said it was a good adaptation of Mackinder's novel.
I think it was, but perhaps the story's time had

finally passed. I always thought the ethos of the
novel was very Forties and Fifties. It worked OK in
1967 but maybe by 2003 'The Fountains of Time'
had lost something of its mystique and dramatic
point.

**I most strongly disagree! It's quite extraordin-
ary, you've been telling me all day what a classic
the book is and after finally persuading me of the
truth of this you're now saying the novel's had
its moment and no longer has the power to thrill
and entertain! A classic novel is just that: a work
of art that can weather changes in style, taste and
fashion, something that can survive when the
time in which it was created is long gone.**

I think the novel is a classic, but I also think the
time when it can be adapted to suit the tastes
of a Twenty-first Century television audience has
now gone. We had nearly twenty million viewers
turning on in 1967, but that you'll remember was
the Summer of Love. Viewers were receptive to a
goodly chunk of mystical philosophy: there was
something rich and strange in the air, it was tangible, you could almost reach out and touch it.
The hippies had the big idea of that decade: love,
peace and doing your own thing. Well, the big
idea died sometime in 1969, and some of us still
mourn that death. By 2003 everything, apart from
the counter-culture's love affair with drugs, had
changed. The great religions had been beaten to
the ground until the only people left who believe

in God are footballers, soap stars and pop singers. Two ghosts in a rose garden talking about the immortality of the soul? I don't think so.

9. EXT. THE ROSE GARDEN. STUDIO. DAY

(IT IS DUSK. THE CHILDREN SIT BETWEEN THE FOUNTAIN SPIRITS ON A BENCH BY THE WALL. MICHAEL IS EXAMINING THE HE-SPIRIT'S DAGGER AND THE SHE-SPIRIT IS PLAITING SUSAN'S HAIR IN SIXTEENTH CENTURY STYLE. THE FOUNTAIN HAS BEEN REPAIRED AND IS ONCE AGAIN SPLASHING WATER INTO THE SCALLOP SHELLS)

MICHAEL: So you see we have to go back to London tomorrow.

SUSAN: I spoke to Daddy on the telephone and begged him to let us stay at Monckton Manor for another week but he said we absolutely had to go on holiday in the Lake District.

MICHAEL: The telephone, incidentally, is a device for talking over long distances.

SHE-SPIRIT: I know what a telephone is, Michael.

MICHAEL: Of course, I'm sorry I forgot – you know everything really don't you!

HE-SPIRIT: We know all that needs to be known.

SUSAN: Did you know that we would finally find the treasure?

MICHAEL: And that it wouldn't be worth enough to do up the Manor so that Uncle Philip and Aunt Julie could open it up to the public?

SUSAN: But it would be worth just enough to repair the fountain.

(THE HE-SPIRIT GIVES HIS SISTER A SHARP GLANCE AND SHE LOOKS AWAY EMBARRASSED)

SHE-SPIRIT: That is the way with treasure seekers, they always complain that the treasure they found is not the treasure they were looking for.

SUSAN: I think we found a much greater treasure than those silly old coins and relics – we found you!

MICHAEL: Yes, of course! Two fantastic ghosts who saved us when we most needed them are much more important than a stupid bag of old treasure.

HE-SPIRIT: You forgive me then for knocking you to the ground in Scotland?

MICHAEL: I didn't mind really.

SHE-SPIRIT: (TO SUSAN) And you forgive me for slapping you?

SUSAN: It really didn't hurt that much.

HE-SPIRIT: Do you know why we so cruel to you?

MICHAEL: I was always doing and saying the wrong things.

SUSAN: And I couldn't stop asking stupid questions.

SHE-SPIRIT: (TAKING SUSAN'S FACE GENTLY IN HER HANDS) Look at me, Susan.

(THE SHE-SPIRIT'S FACE SLOWLY FADES TO BE REPLACED BY SUSAN'S FACE. AMAZED, MICHAEL LOOKS INTO THE HE-SPIRIT'S FACE AND HE TOO SEES HIMSELF IN THE GHOST)

MICHAEL: But you're us!

SUSAN: How can we be you?

HE-SPIRIT: You were always destined to find the treasure because you lost it in the first place! You, Michael and Susan were Sir Roger and Lady Anne de Freece in another life and you have travelled through Time via many different lives until this moment when Time can join the circle and the end and the beginning can be as one.

MICHAEL: Golly!

SHE-SPIRIT: And you were all those people you met on the way as well: Captain Blood and his blousy mistress, Madeleine.

HE-SPIRIT: Beau Brummel and the beautiful Lady

Wellesley.

SHE-SPIRIT: Peter the Painter and poor Maria Trasslonsky.

HE-SPIRIT: And even the horrible Helga Gerdes and Otto Weiss! Good and bad, they were all reflections of yourselves.

SHE-SPIRIT: So if we spirits were cruel to you then we were also being cruel to ourselves.

MICHAEL: But what was all the effort for? Surely not for a canvas bag of religious trinkets?

HE-SPIRIT: Who can say what life and death is for? We know only that the cycle must be always renewed and that we must go on until we find wisdom or wisdom finds us.

SUSAN: Are you saying that we need to live lots of lives, as human beings and as ghosts, and we have to be all different kinds of people – good as well as bad – and that we end up as . . . well what do we end up as?

SHE-SPIRIT: One day when the world was young and only animals lived here something happened.

HE-SPIRIT: The earth was visited by gods and made ready for mankind. A process was put in place whereby man would live on the earth and make his own religions but never know who had really created him.

SHE-SPIRIT: The only marker the gods left to show they had been here at all was the site where they first appeared.

MICHAEL: Where was that?

HE-SPIRIT: You are looking at it, Michael.

SUSAN: The Fountains of Time!

SHE-SPIRIT: (MOVING TOWARDS THE FOUN-TAIN) And now we must return to the world of spirits.

MICHAEL: Will we see you again?

HE-SPIRIT: (ALSO GOING TO THE FOUNTAIN) One day when you are both old and near the end of your lives in this incarnation you will return to Monckton Manor and live here together and be-fore you die we shall all meet again.

SUSAN: We'll never forget you.

MICHAEL: And thank you very much for helping us find the treasure even if it was only enough to repair the fountain.

HE-SPIRIT: Sister!

SHE-SPIRIT: Oh, very well!

(RELUCTANTLY THE SHE-SPIRIT TAKES OFF TWO OF HER MASSIVE RINGS AND WITH A FINAL FOND GLANCE PLACES THEM IN THE CHILDREN'S

HANDS)

HE-SPIRIT: After the time when we escaped with the monks treasure and before Henry's soldier's hacked us to death my sister secreted two of the more valuable pieces.

SHE-SPIRIT: I was safeguarding them, brother dear! I had no intention of keeping the rings for all eternity!

HE-SPIRIT: They have been kept by you very safely for four hundred years and now they must be given to the children.

(THE SHE-SPIRIT PLACES THEM ON THE CHILDREN'S FINGERS AND GIVES EACH CHILD A KISS AND THE HE-SPIRIT KISSES SUSAN AND SHAKES MICHAEL'S HAND)

SHE-SPIRIT: They are extremely valuable, you know.

SUSAN: I shall never part from this for as long as I live.

HE-SPIRIT: I thought you wanted the treasure to give to your aunt and uncle so they could restore their house?

MICHAEL: (GUILTILY) Yes, we did say that, didn't we.

HE-SPIRIT: Then that is what you must do with

the rings. If my sister can relinquish them after twenty lifetimes then so can you after twenty minutes. Good luck Michael and Susan!

(THE SHE-SPIRIT BRIEFLY WAVES FAREWELL AND BOTH GHOSTS FADE BACK INTO THEIR MARBLE REPRESENTATIONS ON THE FOUN-TAINS OF TIME. THE CHILDREN STAND STAR-ING FOR A MOMENT THEN SHOW EACH OTHER THEIR RINGS AND DASH OFF DOWN THE PATH TO FIND THEIR AUNT AND UNCLE)

GRAMS: CLOSING MUSIC AND BRING UP FINAL CREDITS

Wow! You know after watching you and Hédi to-gether in that final scene – how tender and beau-tiful you were together – anyone would have to be crazy to believe that you would go on to murder her five hours later. I guess I was both crazy and extremely stupid to think you could have done such a thing, I'm sorry, Robin.
Oh Gawd, pop goes my million-dollar libel suit!

Yeah, your bloody children's charities can go hang!
I suppose you want me to tell you now what hap-pened that night when Hédi died? I've not told anyone before because I'm not very proud of my-self and really it was nobody else's business. But

you've stayed the course with me here all day,
you've sat and listened to my life and career and
terrible jokes, I suppose I must give you what
you've come for.

**Now I've got my head round the importance of
'The Fountains of Time' in your life, and Hédi's
life, I'm going to write such a brilliant biography
that no one will ever forget you or Hédi again.
With the book and the DVD before the public you
will become the stars and icons you should have
been for the past forty years.**
Terrific! I couldn't give a tuppenny fart for myself
but Hédi deserves her posthumous rehabilitation
enhancing if anyone does, so here goes:

After everyone had returned home after the
recording of that last episode and gone to bed –
me in the spare room — if you remember, I crept
to the telephone and tried to ring Hédi's flat half
a dozen times with no answer – as we know, she
was having a bath. I simply couldn't leave things
the way they were with Hédi storming off the set
like that that so I slipped out and managed to get a
cab to her place where I hung on the doorbell until
she finally condescended to let me in. She was tremendously upset and cross with me for making
her fall in love with yet another married man,
this time one who not only had a delightful wife
but also two incredibly wonderful children. I got
angry too, I told her to grow up: these things happen in life, especially in our show business kind of

life and that she should face the problem maturely
and stop behaving like a twenty-five year old virgin.

Actually she probably was a virgin.
Eh?

**According to my researches there's absolutely no
evidence that she ever slept around or indeed as
far as I can tell, slept with anyone.**
Good God! I thought I was beyond such surprises.
What about this bloke Toby or Tony she'd been
mooning over before I came along?

**Whatever happened between them certainly
wasn't sexual. I think for all her beauty perhaps
she was rather timid when it came to men. From
what I gather after reading her diaries he was
more of a fantasy figure for Hédi than a real lover.
They dated a few times, went to concerts and the
opera, but it's obvious that he was a typically re-
served Englishman who was never going to leave
his wife or leap into some passionate affair with
a movie actress. It's funny, we don't have too
many guys like that in the States.**
No I don't suppose you do. There again I don't suppose you have too many twenty-five year old film
actresses who are virgins either.

True.
Anyway I told Hédi straight: I was moving out of
the family home in the morning and consulting a
solicitor about divorce proceedings. I wasn't pre-

pared to live my life without her and I would make a complete and utter arse of myself until she agreed to marry me.

What did she say to that?
She laughed and accepted my proposal of marriage.

Sounds more like a proposal of blackmail to me.
Yes it was really wasn't it? But if you'll forgive the appalling sexist remark, sometimes girls like Hédi need their minds making up for them. I think she did love me and she knew I wouldn't let her go. I was bloody impressed with her concern for Christine and the children – how many girls these days would be bothered by a little thing like that? – but my marriage was dead and every soul on this earth has an entitlement to happiness. I would have done anything for Christine and the children to mitigate any hardship they would suffer but Hédi and I were made for each other and we had to be together.

So how did the two of you end up in the Citroen?
It was incredibly late and Hédi agreed to run me home. The old Traction-Avant may have zipped around Paris in the Maigret programmes but it wasn't really that fast and I don't suppose Hedi was doing much more than forty when the accident happened. It was about two in the morning and we were heading along the Embankment and because it was a freezing cold night there wasn't

another car or pedestrian to be seen. We were talking about something quite inconsequential – I've never been able to remember what it was – then Hédi suddenly turned to look at me; and it was extremely odd because for one split second I thought I was looking at the face of Billie Gibson.

Not that dreadful minx again!
It was very dark in the car apart from the yellow glare from the Embankment lights every few seconds and in one of these brief moments of illumination I thought I was sitting next to Billie and then in the next it was Hédi again. It was extraordinary because Hédi looked absolutely nothing like Billie Gibson and I hadn't even thought about her for ages, certainly never put the two actresses together in my mind even though they had played the same role in 'The Fountains of Time'.

Did you say anything to Hedi?
No, she spoke to me and said something very odd.

'You know I will always love you, Roger.'

She called you Roger instead of Robin?
Slip of the tongue I suppose but it unsettled me then and for some reason has continued to do so ever since.

She was thinking of Sir Roger de Freece in 'The Fountains of Time' – it was a temporary mental throwback to the part you'd just been playing.
Probably.

But I've seen that name in this room in another context. Now where was it?

5.0-5.30 CHILDREN'S TELEVISION

The Fountains of Time
A serial in six parts
from the book by
Adrian Mackinder

Adapted and produced
for television
by Patrick Keith

1. 'The Mystery of Monckton Manor'

Mr Summerwood............…..........Norman Hughes
Mrs Summerwood............…......….......Mary Lester
Their children:
Michael ....…............ ....Robin Glass
Susan ....…...................... ....Anna Lombard
Uncle Philip...................…...…...............Claude Irving
Aunt Julie................................…....…........Blanche Bayless
Stationmaster........... ….….......William Fleming
Old Daniel....................…...…........Lawrence England
He-Spirit...................................…...…...........Roger Blake
She-Spirit...................................…...…..........Billie Gibson

Settings by Gordon Carson

Roger Blake! He played opposite Billie Gibson when you were Michael in 1954.
So he did! Hédi couldn't have known anything about him playing my part thirteen years earlier,

could she?

You never mentioned this to her?
Why should I have done? If you remember I was
keeping very quiet about Lawrence England pop-
ping his clogs in Billie Gibson's dressing room, so
all chat about the 1954 production of 'The Fountains of Time' was strictly verboten as far as I was
concerned.

**And you told me how Shelley Fox, playing Susan
in 2002 called the Stuffed-Shirt bimbo acting the
She-spirit, 'Hédi' – another slip of the tongue.**
And another coincidence?

**You say Hédi appeared to you in a split second as
Billie Gibson, then called you 'Roger'. As well as
servicing Lawrence England, could she also have
had a fling with Roger Blake?**
It's possible I suppose, but I don't like to think it
could be true. Blake died a few years ago so now
we'll never know.

Anyway, the crash happened soon after all this?
Almost immediately. Without any warning Hédi
swung the Citroen up onto the pavement and we
ran into a tree at forty miles an hour. I had just
enough time to lean over and make a grab at the
steering wheel – hence those fingerprints at 270
degrees – but we hit before I could straighten the
car. I was half lying across the seat so struck the
dashboard and took most of the impact on my
arms and shoulders. With no seat belts in the car

Hédi hit the windscreen and died immediately.

How do you know that?

I could see she was dead. There wasn't a mark on her face but her eyes were fully open and completely devoid of life. Her chest wasn't moving, she'd stopped breathing. All I wanted to do was get out of the car. I suppose I must have been quite badly concussed but I could see a bench on the Embankment overlooking the river and my first thought was to make for it so I could lie down and stop myself from fainting. I must have passed out immediately because when I awoke about two hours later completely stiff and frozen to the bone I looked around and to my amazement both Hédi and the car had vanished.

Jesus!

I hobbled over to the tree and could see the newly stripped bark and the bits of broken glass in the road but the car had completely disappeared.

The police had towed it away.

And hadn't noticed me slumped on the embankment bench fifty yards along from the accident! Anyway I felt well enough to walk the rest of the journey home and decided that I would contact the police in the morning. I realise now I must have been in a state of total shock. I remember nothing about that walk home or going to bed. The next thing I knew was pulling the 'Daily Mirror' from the letterbox and reading that Hédi had been killed in a car crash in the early hours of the morning. It was then that I went to pieces because I knew that I'd lost her forever.

How did Christine react to the news?

By not gloating over the death of her rival and by being very kind to me. Of course she was unaware that I'd been in the car at the time or perhaps she wouldn't have been quite so sympathetic. She sent the kids to her mother's and sent me back to bed with some warm milk and two pink tablets – God knows where she'd got them from. I duly passed out again and didn't wake for another twenty-four hours.

And then you found you had a problem.

I hadn't been to the police.

And you saw there were considerable advantages in not going to the police.

Huge advantages. Hédi appeared to have died alone, by placing myself next to her in the car there would be scandal, scandal, scandal. Scandal first of all for Hédi's memory: what was she doing driving along the Embankment with her co-star at two in the morning? Why hadn't he immediately gone to the police and reported the accident? He was stretched out on a bench fifty yards away and didn't hear the police arrive? Why didn't he report the accident when he got home? Why didn't he report the accident when he got up the next morning? Any statement I made to the police at that late stage would stink to high heaven. Then there was the scandal that would fall on Christine and the children. Did they deserve to go through all that? What was the bloody point of my going to the police and causing so much distress to three perfectly innocent people?

What was the point of your going to the police and ruining your acting career?
OK, fair comment, there was that too, but it was way down my list of priorities. When Hédi died my acting career was very far from my thoughts, in fact I wouldn't have given a stuff if I'd never acted again. Show business trades in dreams, when real tragedy comes along the tinsel can seem extremely tawdry. I had lost the woman I was in love with. If I hadn't cadged a lift home from her that night but called a cab instead she would still be alive. I felt a huge sense of guilt and responsibility for her death but above all was the unbelievable and quite unacceptable notion that I would never see Hédi again. Jesus, I would never see Hédi again!

Do you think she was trying to kill you when she drove into that tree?
No, why on earth should she? And I don't think it was a suicide attempt either, Hédi simply wasn't the type. Something odd happened in that car immediately before the accident. Suddenly the atmosphere seemed changed and quite different. I think in that instant Hédi thought she was somewhere else. Driving alone perhaps or with some-

one else along a different road. Maybe she saw something in the road she tried to avoid or perhaps she believed she was taking a sharp bend. I've no idea, but I haven't got over her death, you know. Not a single day has gone by without me thinking of her and although the last forty years have certainly had periods of considerable contentment, I can put my hand on my heart and say that I have not experienced a moment of real happiness since the day she died.

Did you attend the funeral in January, '68?
Wasn't invited. Her mother had the body flown back to Hungry and Hédi was buried in her birthtown of Tamasi. I've visited her grave several times since then, it's nothing much to look at but it has been well cared for. I have a photograph of the gravestone somewhere, if I can lay my hands on it. Oh, this is even better: my favourite portrait of Hédi and me taken together.

Jeez, Robin, I've not seen this one before, it's perfectly charming!
It was taken on the set of Beau Brummel's parlour by a BBC photographer. I don't think it was ever published but he kindly gave me a copy. As you can see we're both in mufti. Hédi had this marvellous quality of looking very natural, even ordinary, when she wasn't 'on'. I like this photo particularly because it shows her basic niceness.

It does. But more than that it shows the pair of

you on the edge of falling in love.

Yes, I think you're absolutely right. I hadn't thought about it before but I suppose we must have taped the Beau Brummel scene very shortly afterwards. I certainly look cheerful enough – talk about living in a bloody fool's paradise! Hard to imagine that within three weeks Hédi would be dead.

Would it be possible for me to borrow this photograph, Robin?

Certainly. Thinking of using it as an illustration in your biography?

I think I'd like to have this image on the cover actually.

Good Lord, fame at last! Ah, but perhaps you were thinking of cropping me and just leaving Hédi?

No! I want to keep both of you exactly the way you are. 'The Fountains of Time' is your story too, Robin. But then it was always your story: Hédi Gela blundered into the enchantment of Adrian Mackinder's novel by accident simply because Anna Lombard didn't want to act in the serial. Perhaps after all Anna was smarter than you gave her credit for.

Don't think so! I believe that Hédi was always destined to be in the show. She was a wonderfully accomplished actress who would certainly have gone on to great things and would have won all kinds of awards and reached the very top of her profession. I don't think it would have spoiled her because she was not that sort of person. I believe if we had married we would have become a great team and had a brilliant life together. We would have continued to work professionally and done some good stuff and I would most certainly have also more completely fulfilled my talent and ambition. But I've not done so badly on my own and at least we were both together in 'The Fountains of Time'.

Michael and Susan enjoyed their holiday among the streams, valleys and mountains of the Lake District, even though it seemed to rain very nearly every day. Their father had been tremendously successful in France and had managed to get his wartime friend released from prison with all the charges dropped. Both Father and Mother therefore were in excellent spirits and did all they could, in spite of the terrible weather, to see the children had a happy holiday. They felt sorry for them having had to spend three rather boring weeks in Devon while they themselves had had such an exciting time in France talking to the police and lots of different lawyers and attending court hearings. Perhaps they should have taken the children with them after all for they would surely have loved driving through the beautiful lanes in the French countryside seeing their father interviewing witnesses and hunting down the evidence that would finally release his friend from an unjust imprisonment.

It's true the children had apparently found some rather valuable rings hidden in the rose garden together with some religious relics and these were likely to be declared 'treasure trove' which would apparently help Philip and Julie to restore Monckton Manor to something like its former glory. It was nice of Michael and Susan to give up their find so readily and not want anything in return for themselves.

But it was odd, somehow in the three weeks they had been away in Devon, the children had changed. How, it was rather difficult to say. Michael no longer seemed interested in talking much about finding treasure. Well, he'd found some, hadn't he? It's perfectly natural to loose interest in something after a goal has been achieved. It was good that he would now go on to develop other interests. And Susan? Why, she'd completely stopped talking about ghosts! Now that was a very funny thing! A month ago all you ever saw Susan doing was reading ghost stories, and now she given all her ghost books away. Well that was to the good too, about time the girl read something decent for a change rather than all that ghost and horror rubbish.

But the children had definitely become slightly different in some tiny but rather peculiar way. It was very odd.

Michael loved the Lake District and was pleased that his parents seemed so cheerful and that Susan had become much more grown up since their adventure with the Fountains of Time. He was proud of her for being so brave when things hadn't gone their way and he was glad that having met two real ghosts she no longer seemed interested in imaginary ones who only lived in books.

But he found himself thinking about ghosts a great deal. He couldn't get out of his mind the last thing the Fountain Spirit had said to him about Susan and himself ending their lives living together at Monckton Manor where they might then see the ghosts once more. He didn't at all mind the idea of ending up living at Monckton Manor with his sister – he loved Susan, he loved the old house and the idea that Uncle Philip and Aunt Julie would one day leave the property to them was heart-warming and something surely to be looked forward to, but . . .

There was no possible reason why anyone should object to such an outcome in their lives but somehow Michael felt unhappy about the prospect. It was the certainty that this was going to happen that he found so unsettling. Whatever he might do or achieve in his life – good things, bad things, wonderful things, stupid things, interesting things, dull things, he would always end up living at Monckton Manor with his sister. There simply was no getting out of it. The ghosts had never lied to them so why should they be lying now? Michael couldn't help wishing that the ghosts had kept this small piece of divination to themselves so he could get on with his life like everyone else without knowing what was going to happen in the end.

Susan also found herself troubled by something the ghosts had said. She remembered them telling the children that they were the ghosts and the ghosts were them. It seemed such a silly idea at the time but the more Susan thought about it the more true such an odd statement seemed to be. She caught herself looking at Michael when he was unaware of her staring at him and it was simply astounding how sometimes he appeared to look like a much younger version of the He-spirit. He had those same eyes that could glint with fun and amusement one minute but gleam with a steely cruelty the next. She had liked and admired the He-spirit in many ways but she was not so sure that she wished her brother to turn into him.

And what of herself? Was she destined to become the regal and haughty She-spirit? The ghost had been extremely beautiful it was true, but what of her sullen silences and temper tantrums? Was this the creature that Susan was destined to become? She would sometimes sit at her dressing room mirror and look at her reflection staring back at her. Were those the large shinning eyes of Lady Anne de Freece? Should she let her hair tumble down in heavy black curls like a wild gypsy's? Would she be afraid to ever have it cut short like the She-Spirit? What would happen if she closed her eyes and concentrated very, very hard and then opened them suddenly to gaze once again into the mirror. Whose face would she see looking back at her?

The End

ABOUT THE AUTHOR

David Phillips

was born in Leicester and grew up in South London, before moving to Margate in 1979 to take up a teaching post. He has now retired.

The move to Kent's creative hub proved providential to his writing. David has had poems and articles published in many magazines including Poetry Review, The Spectator and Classical Recordings Quarterly. His prize winning poetry extolling the virtues of Newcastle Brown Ale has featured on the London Underground, and his radio plays have been aired by the BBC and RTE.

www.margatepoet.co.uk

BOOKS BY THIS AUTHOR

Man In The Long Grass

Marjorie Walk

Selected Poems

Gigantika

Printed in Great Britain
by Amazon